# The Battle for the Worlds

# The Battle for the Worlds
## BOOK ONE OF THE TARLIAN SPIRAL
## HAROLD B. BULLOCK

ILLUSTRATION BY PAIGE MENEFEE

Edited by Jean Anderson

THE SUMMIT GROUP
FORT WORTH, TEXAS

PUBLISHED BY

THE SUMMIT GROUP

1227 WEST MAGNOLIA

FORT WORTH, TEXAS 76104

Library of Congress Cataloging in Publication Data

**Bullock, Harold B.**
The battle for the worlds: book one of The Tarlian spiral /
Harold B. Bullock. –
p. cm. – (The Tarlian spiral; book 1)

SUMMARY: In 1930s America, Mark Woods encounters beings
from another world who have come to reclaim a stone with
supernatural powers.
ISBN 0-9626219-4-3

1. {Fantasy.} I. Title. II. Series: Bullock, Harold B.
Tarlian spiral; book 1.

PZ7      813.54

LCCN: 90-71802

MARC

Printed in the United States of America

# Contents

CHAPTER ONE    ❖ *The Unexpected Entry* . . . . *PAGE 3*

CHAPTER TWO    ❖ *The Supernatural Marble*. . *PAGE 11*

CHAPTER THREE    ❖ *The Watcher* . . . . . . . . . . . *PAGE 19*

CHAPTER FOUR    ❖ *The Chest of Gold* . . . . . . . *PAGE 27*

CHAPTER FIVE    ❖ *In Outer Space* . . . . . . . . . *PAGE 37*

CHAPTER SIX    ❖ *The Night Visitor* . . . . . . . . *PAGE 45*

CHAPTER SEVEN    ❖ *Kintras of Stargis-Lin* . . . . *PAGE 53*

CHAPTER EIGHT    ❖ *The Unseen Flaw* . . . . . . . . *PAGE 61*

CHAPTER NINE    ❖ *The Fate of the Worlds* . . . *PAGE 69*

CHAPTER TEN    ❖ *The Stone of Darkness* . . . *PAGE 79*

CHAPTER ELEVEN    ❖ *The Wall of Terror* . . . . . . . *PAGE 87*

CHAPTER TWELVE    ❖ *Desperate Plans* . . . . . . . . *PAGE 95*

CHAPTER THIRTEEN    ❖ *The Dagger's Work* . . . . . . *PAGE 103*

CHAPTER FOURTEEN    ❖ *The Return* . . . . . . . . . . . . *PAGE 111*

ILLUSTRATION BY PATTI SMITH

# The Battle for the Worlds

✧

# The Unexpected Entry

**M**ARK WOODS sat at his desk, gazing through the open window before him. He propped his chin in his hands, looking at the small red barn below. Two chattering squirrels chased around and around on the barn roof. "Squirrels sure are lucky," Mark said to himself. "They get to play all day and they don't have to do homework."

He glanced down at his math book and homework papers and sighed. Mother had told him to finish quickly, so he knew he had better get back to work. He picked up his pencil. "Four divided by twenty-seven," he mumbled, copying the numbers onto the paper. "Zero, decimal point – whaaaa!"

Suddenly a small, glistening object shot across the desk. It grazed his hand and rolled across the floor. Mark jumped up and scrambled after it. He caught a glimpse of the object as it rolled under his bed and whacked the wall.

Kneeling beside the bed, he lifted the fringe of the bed-spread and cautiously peered underneath. Several inches from the wall lay a marble. Mark crawled under the bed and retrieved it. Then he walked back to his desk.

"Mark, are you doing your homework or playing?" came Mother's voice up the stairs and through his open door. "I thought I heard something rolling over the floor."

"A marble rolled off my desk," Mark answered. "I'll get right back to work!"

"Get your homework finished quickly," said Mother. "There's not enough firewood for breakfast. Since we are leaving for church right after we eat dinner tonight, you need to cut some wood before we eat."

"I will, Momma."

The rays of the late afternoon sun streamed through the window, across Mark's desk. Opening his hand in the sunlight, he studied the marble.

He had never seen such a marble! It was clear with gold and silver flecks in it. In the sunshine it sparkled like a huge diamond. Rainbows of colored light reflected on the walls of his room and danced about as Mark turned the marble over in his palm.

Mark stared at the marble, amazed at its beauty. Then his forehead wrinkled in thought. How did the marble shoot across his desk? He knew it wasn't on his desk when he sat down to do his homework. "I bet one of the guys threw it through the window!" he said aloud.

Mark put the marble in his pocket, climbed up onto the desk and stuck his head out the window. From his window on the second floor he could see the whole backyard. The grass was getting tall enough to cut, and the flowers next to the house were blooming.

Trace, Mark's big, black pup, was lying in the yard. Mark looked down at the back porch but saw no one. He glanced over toward the barn but saw no one–even the squirrels were gone.

"Trace would have barked if someone came into the yard," he thought. "And besides, the marble didn't drop on the desk and roll off; it shot straight across the desk."

He climbed off the desk and slumped in his chair, puzzled. Then he got up and carefully inspected the raised wooden rim around the sides and back of the desk. No holes. Nothing.

He dug the marble out of his pocket and held it between his fingers, watching it sparkle and scatter color.

"Wow! Momma's got to see this!" He ran out the bedroom door and down the stairs.

From the kitchen came the fresh, sweet smell of bread baking – and the voice of President Roosevelt. Mother always liked to listen to the radio as she worked in the kitchen. But she usually didn't like to be interrupted when the president was making a speech.

Mark paused in the doorway. Mother had her back to him, and she was stirring something on the stove. Her brown hair was tied back with a scarf.

Although she was busy and listening to the president, Mark decided she'd want to know about the mysterious appearance of the marble.

"Look at this, Momma!" he exclaimed, running into the kitchen.

"What, darling?" she asked, turning around.

"Look!" said Mark. He stood by the window overlooking the backyard, and opened his fist so the sun's rays would strike the marble.

"Why, Mark – it's beautiful!" she exclaimed. "Where did

you get it?" She took a dishtowel from the table by the stove and wiped her hands. Then she turned down the radio.

"You're not going to believe this," he warned, "but, honest, it's the truth!"

"Why should I think you'd lie, Mark?" she asked, walking over to him.

"Because this is the strangest thing that's ever happened to me!"

Mother took the marble and held it in the sunlight. Rainbow colors danced on her full white apron and on the room around them.

"Well, tell me about it," she prompted.

Mark explained what had happened a few minutes earlier, and that he couldn't figure out how the marble had entered his room.

Mother handed the marble back to Mark. "Let's go look together," she said. They went upstairs, pulled the desk from the wall and looked around.

"Mark, are you telling me the truth?" Momma asked.

"See, I told you that you wouldn't believe me," he moaned in a despairing voice.

"Mark, look me in the eyes!" she said seriously.

Mark lifted his eyes to her clear, steady brown eyes. "Are you telling me the truth?"

"Yes, ma'am," he answered quietly.

"Then I believe you. I don't understand this, but I believe you.

"Now, finish your homework quickly," she said. "Put the marble in your pocket. Dr. Taylor should be at the meeting tonight. We'll ask him about it after church. But hurry, supper will be ready soon."

Dr. Taylor was a longtime friend of the family and the only

physician in town. To Mark, the doctor looked just like the president of the United States should, only younger. He was tall and broad-shouldered with a kind face and gray hair.

Mark liked Dr. Taylor a lot. The doctor had always noticed him and been nice to him. And, Dr. Taylor always had a peppermint or two in his vest pocket for children!

After dinner they quickly cleared the table and started for church. Since it would be dark when they returned, Mother turned on the porch light as they left. The walk to church took about twenty minutes. Along the road leading into town, signs of spring were everywhere; yellow and purple spring flowers bloomed in the front yards they passed. The trees were covered with fresh green leaves. Busy birds flitted about collecting twigs and things for their nests. Several school friends waved to them as they walked along the road.

When the church meeting was over, Mother went to speak to Dr. Taylor. Mark ran outside to play with the other children. A bit later he saw Mother and the doctor come outside and stand talking under a large tree.

After several minutes Mother called Mark and motioned for him to come over to them.

"Mark, could I see this mysterious marble of yours?" Dr. Taylor asked with a smile. He held out his hand.

"Yes, sir," said Mark. Mark dropped the marble into the doctor's large, open hand. Even in the dim light outside the church building the marble glistened. Rainbows of color danced on the three of them, the ground below and the tree branches above. The doctor rolled the marble around in his open palm, studying it.

"You have never seen the marble before, Mark?" asked the doctor, still examining it.

"No, sir," answered Mark, "not until this afternoon."

"And the marble just shot across your desk?"

"Yes, sir. From the back of my desk."

"Thank you, Mark." he said with a smile. "You can go back and play with your friends again."

Mark heard the doctor say something about "three explanations" as he ran to play. Mother and Dr. Taylor talked a while longer. Then she called Mark again.

"Dr. Taylor is giving us a ride home," she said. "Dust yourself off and come along."

Mark got into the back seat of the doctor's shiny black car. The 1938 Buick was the only brand-new car in town. Mother rode in the front beside the doctor. She and the doctor were silent on the brief ride home. Mark ran his hands over the smooth, gray leather seats. He inhaled deeply, enjoying the smell of the new car.

In a few minutes they pulled up in front of Mark's home. He wished they lived farther out from town so the ride could have lasted longer.

Mrs. Woods turned toward the doctor and smiled. "Thank you, Jim. You've been a great help. And I won't hesitate to call on you."

Dr. Taylor got out, went around the car and opened Mother's door. But Mark opened his own door and ran for the front porch. Trace came bounding up the porch after him, barking and wagging his tail. Mark scratched Trace's ears while Dr. Taylor walked Mother up onto the porch. She opened the front door and turned back around to face the doctor. "Thank you again, Jim," she said.

"You are more than welcome, Madelyn," replied Dr. Taylor. He put his hand into his right coat pocket and then drew it out again. "Goodnight, Mark," he said, offering his hand for a handshake.

"Goodnight, sir," Mark said. He shook the doctor's hand. And he felt something small, round and flat in the doctor's palm.

"Take good care of your mother!" said Dr. Taylor with a wink. Mark quietly took the flat object in his fingers and put his hand down to his side.

"Goodnight, Madelyn," smiled Dr. Taylor, as he turned and went down the steps.

While the doctor walked to his car Mark glanced down to the flat object in his right hand. Through his slightly opened fingers he saw red swirls on a white background. It was a peppermint!

With a big grin on his face Mark waved at the doctor. Dr. Taylor returned the wave.

"Remember," he called, "if strange things start happening, let me know!"

He got in the car and drove away.

# The Supernatural Marble

MOTHER TURNED to go into the house. Mark popped the peppermint into his mouth and followed her inside. Trace came in behind him, sniffing at his shoes and pants, curious about the interesting scents Mark had brought home. His hunter's nose twitched back and forth.

Once inside Mark burst out, "Something really great happened tonight after church!"

"What, Mark?" Mother asked, setting her purse on the piano in the parlor.

"I didn't miss a shot with Shiner!" Mark grinned.

"What do you mean, Mark?"

"Marbles, Momma!" he answered. "You know! I played with Dan, Billy and Randy after church. And I couldn't miss with Shiner, here!" He took the glistening marble from his pocket and tossed it jauntily in one hand.

"You didn't miss a single shot?" she questioned closely.

"I did once, ma'am," answered Mark seriously. "I used my old favorite, Red Eye, and I missed. But then I started using my new marble, Shiner, and I couldn't miss. I knocked all the marbles out of the ring! I didn't miss a shot!"

"Not once?" she asked again.

"No ma'am, not once," he answered, looking her in the eye.

"Well, that fits." For a moment Mother stared over Mark's head, thinking.

"What fits, Momma?" wondered Mark.

"How good a marble player are you normally, Mark?" she asked, still looking off into space.

"Oh, about average," he answered. "It's Billy Wilder who's really good."

Suddenly she looked at him sternly. "You didn't play 'for keeps,' did you?"

"No, ma'am. Everyone got their marbles back."

Mother felt playing for keeps was gambling. Mark knew better than to play for keeps.

"But what fits, Momma?"

"Come here," she beckoned. She put her arms around him and pulled him close. "Mark, you know I love you. And I do not believe you have lied to me. But in this situation there is something I need to do.

"I believe you about not missing in marbles. But I'm going to call Billy's mom and ask about your game. You put Trace outside and get ready for bed. After I've talked to Mrs. Wilder, I'll come up and tell you why I called her."

"Okay, Momma," said Mark.

Mother went into the kitchen to make the phone call.

"C'mon, Trace!" said Mark, starting for the front door. Trace trotted happily after him and went outside.

Mother was still talking on the phone when Mark went up to dress for bed. He had finished brushing his teeth and was climbing into bed when Mother came into the room, smiling.

"Mrs. Wilder said that Billy was angry all the way home because you didn't miss a single shot after your first one," she said as she sat down on the bed beside him.

"See, I was telling the truth," said Mark. "But what is it that fits, Momma?"

"Well, it's like this." Mother began to explain. "I talked to Dr. Taylor and told him about the marble. He said that if you were telling the truth and the marble had shot off the desk, but we had found no way for it to get into the room and onto the desk, then there were only three possible explanations.

"One, the marble had come from somewhere in this world by scientific process. Two, it had come from another world by alien science. Or third, it came by a supernatural process which is unexplainable according to the laws of nature.

"And he said that, whichever explanation was correct, there would probably be other unusual or unexplainable things happening.

"So, your not missing your shots with Shiner – that fits!" said Mother. "It's something out of the ordinary!"

"Wow!" exclaimed Mark. He thought for a moment. "Did Dr. Taylor say which one of the three explanations he thought was the right one?"

Mother's face took on a very serious look as she straightened the bed covers. "He said that the science of our own world couldn't make a marble appear in someone's room. He thinks we are either dealing with science from another world or with the supernatural.

"I asked him what he meant about the supernatural," she continued. "He told me that fifteen years ago he served as a doctor with the English army in Africa. While there he saw things happen in the tribes that could only be called supernatural."

"What kind of things?" asked Mark, his eyes wide.

"He wouldn't tell me specific things," Mother answered. "But the things he had seen definitely convinced him that the supernatural was real."

"Space aliens or the supernatural! Wow!"

"Yes," said Mother. "I asked him what advice he would have for us. He said an old missionary in Africa had told him that, when dealing with the supernatural, you needed to pray for wisdom, keep a pure heart, and double-check all your facts. That's why I called Mrs. Wilder – to double-check the facts."

"That's okay, Momma," said Mark. "I understand. But what does Dr. Taylor mean when he says, 'keep a pure heart'?"

"He means not to let lying, greed, pride, or things like that pile up in our hearts. When you see it happening, stop it."

"But why now?" Mark asked. "I mean, what's that got to do with Shiner?"

A serious look came over her face. She looked down at him nestled on the pillow and put her hand on his head. "Darling, if Shiner is from the supernatural, then it is either from the good supernatural or from the bad. And as things continue to happen, unless our hearts are pure, we're going to have a hard time telling which one it is."

In their bedtime prayers, they asked for wisdom and for pure hearts. Then Mother kissed him, turned out the light and closed the door.

Mark's mind was racing. A marble from another world! Or maybe from the supernatural! He couldn't wait to tell the kids at school tomorrow!

Of course he would have to wait until recess. He couldn't whisper in class – Mother was his teacher. But would the kids be surprised!

The supernatural. Wow! The supernatural. Oh, no!

Mark suddenly remembered that Mother had said there were two kinds of supernatural. Mark pulled his bed covers up under his chin. He looked around his room. Things seemed to be awfully dark.

Who knew what kinds of ugly, evil things might suddenly appear in the darkness of his room during the night! Mark wished that Trace were sleeping inside tonight. He got up quickly and opened the door into the dark hall.

It was hard for a boy who was almost ten to ask, but Mark decided his situation was desperate.

"Momma, can we leave the hall light on and my door open tonight?" he called from the hall.

"Of course, darling," her voice came back from her bedroom with a hint of a smile.

"I love you, Momma," he called as he turned on the hall light.

"And I love you," she called back. "Goodnight."

The next day, while Mother was comforting a little girl who had fallen down in the school yard, another teacher walked up to her. "Mrs. Woods," said the teacher, "I think your son Mark may be getting into trouble." She pointed across the school yard where a group of boys was gathering rapidly.

"Thank you, Miss Carpenter," Mother said. She gave the child one final hug and the girl ran off to play. Mother then walked over to the group of boys.

In the middle of the group a boy yelled in Mark's face.

"You're a lousy cheat, Mark Woods!" Mark looked bewildered.

"What's going on here?" demanded Mrs. Woods. All of the children became very quiet.

"Mark cheated at marbles!" blurted out the angry one, a boy named Leroy.

"Mark, look me in the eyes." Mrs. Woods commanded. Mark turned to face her and looked up. "Did you cheat at marbles?" she asked in a solemn voice.

"No, ma'am," he answered, his voice and his eyes level.

She turned to Leroy. "Leroy, look me in the eyes." Leroy looked up, then down. "Look at me, Leroy," she said. Leroy lifted his eyes to meet Mrs. Woods's eyes.

"Did Mark cheat at marbles?"

"Yes," he answered, looking down quickly.

"Look me in the eyes, Leroy, until I tell you to stop!" Mrs. Woods ordered sternly.

Leroy looked up reluctantly and gritted his teeth.

"Did Mark cheat at marbles?" she asked again.

The pupils of Leroy's eyes dilated and shrank. He took a deep breath, his nostrils flared, he fidgeted – but he didn't move his eyes!

"No, ma'am," he said quietly – and then angrily, "But he did use his supernatural marble!"

Mother suddenly realized that, in the rush to get ready and make it to school on time, she had not discussed with Mark what to tell others about the mysterious new marble.

"What happened, Leroy?" Mrs. Woods asked.

Leroy told how he and four other boys had been playing marbles. They had put their marbles in a ring when Mark walked up, bragging that he had a supernatural marble and couldn't miss a shot. They didn't believe him, so they let him put some marbles into the ring. And just to show him up, they had let him go first.

So Mark had pulled out Shiner – and he didn't miss a single shot! Each time he had taken aim and shot his new marble at one of the other marbles, Shiner had knocked the marble out of the ring. And no, they hadn't been playing for "keeps." They had returned all the marbles to their owners.

"What makes you think the marble is supernatural, Leroy?" questioned Mrs. Woods.

"Well, ma'am, can't nobody hit every shot like that, not even Billy Wilder."

The bell ending recess rang.

"Did every one get their marbles back?" Mrs. Woods asked again, to make sure that they had not played for keeps. Heads nodded up and down. "We will discuss this incident further at recess this afternoon."

As the children lined up to go back into the building, Mark stood in line, tossing Shiner up and down with one hand. He had a smirk on his face.

"Mark Woods, put away your marble!" said Mrs. Woods.

Mark quickly obeyed.

Word about the "supernatural marble" spread quickly through the school. By late morning students weren't paying attention to their schoolwork. Notes and whispers passed back and forth behind the teachers' backs in every classroom. All the children talked about the same thing: Mark Woods and his supernatural marble.

At lunch time Mrs. Woods sat with several other teachers in the large lunch room which also served as the town meeting hall. The supernatural marble quickly surfaced as the main topic of conversation. Mrs. Woods told them about the mysterious arrival of the marble and what Dr. Taylor had said.

"For some reason, it is very hard for Mark to miss when

he plays marbles with this new one," she said.

"Well, it definitely has the attention of all the children," commented the sixth grade teacher. "I'm having a terrible time trying to get them to concentrate on their work."

"It's the same in my class," said another teacher. The others agreed.

A commotion across the room caused all of them to turn and look. Mark Woods was heading toward the door into the school yard, tossing Shiner in his right hand. Mrs. Woods could see a smirk on his face. The rest of the boys scooted their chairs back to follow Mark out into the yard.

A red-haired boy in Mark's class, Ned Shipley, was several feet in front of Mark and made it to the screen door first. He went through the door and stood outside holding the door open for Mark. But when Mark got to the door, Ned let the screen door go, and it slammed into Mark.

Ned ran off. Mark stumbled back from the door, regained his composure and then pushed it open, walking through with a slight swagger. The mob of boys streamed out the door behind Mark, talking excitedly.

"I have had trouble with talking and note-passing, too," said Mrs. Woods. "But the thing that is concerning me more and more is the effect this marble is having on Mark. I think it's turning his head and heart in the wrong direction. He's acting more arrogant by the hour."

The teachers discussed how to handle the situation in their classrooms. Finally they decided on a marble-shooting exhibition.

Right after lunch all the teachers announced to their classes that there would be a marble-shooting exhibition during afternoon recess. At that time all the students would be able to see the supernatural marble in action.

## The Watcher

ITH THE exhibition promised, the children settled down and classwork went smoothly.

At recess all the children and teachers lined up in a great half-circle on the playground. The front row of children sat, the middle row knelt or squatted, and the back row stood so that all could see. Teachers stood along the back row with the taller children.

Mrs. Woods walked to the front center of the half-circle and stood near a patch of bare ground. "I'd like Billy Wilder, Leroy Grimes and Mark Woods to join me here," she announced in a loud voice.

The boys walked up to her side. "Billy, would you please draw a ring for marbles on the ground for us? Make it a big ring. And when you're finished, scatter these twenty marbles around the center of it."

She held out a small sack of marbles which Billy took. He picked up a twig lying nearby and drew a large circle on the ground between Mrs. Woods and the watching children. The circle was about four feet across.

While he was drawing, Mrs. Woods spoke again. "We're here this afternoon for a demonstration in marble-shooting. Mark Woods has a supernatural marble. We're going to show how supernatural it is by letting Mark, Billy and Leroy shoot with it. Can any child at this school hit twenty shots in a row?"

A sixth-grader yelled back, "Until this morning I would've said no!"

The rest of the children cheered their agreement.

"First," said Mrs. Woods, "Mark Woods will shoot, then Billy Wilder, then Leroy Grimes. Mark Woods up first!" Mrs. Woods, Billy, and Leroy backed away from the ring to give Mark room.

Mark stepped to the side of the ring opposite the crowd. He took Shiner out of his pocket and held it in the palm of his right hand. For a few seconds he waited, letting the marble glisten in the sun. He had everyone's attention, and he was enjoying it.

Then he knelt down with the marble between his thumb and forefinger, ready to shoot. He put the knuckles of his right hand on the ground and fired. Shiner struck a marble near the center of the ring and the marble flew out of the ring!

Mark shot again and again. Each time Shiner struck a marble in the ring, the marble flew outside the circle. As the number mounted to thirteen, then fourteen, the crowd grew quiet. Mark loved it. In the hush he posed more dramatically and paused before each shot.

Eighteen, nineteen, twenty! The audience yelled and

whistled. As he walked back to Mother, Mark felt ten feet tall. He handed Shiner to Billy Wilder and then ran to return the other marbles into the ring.

Billy walked up to the edge of the ring, knelt down and began shooting. One, two, three. Marble after marble jumped out of the ring as he shot with Shiner.

Eighteen, nineteen, twenty! The crowd cheered but not quite as loudly as before. Since Billy was the best marble player in the whole school, they had expected him to do well.

Billy walked over to Leroy Grimes and gave Shiner to him. Then Billy ran to gather the scattered marbles.

Leroy walked up to the circle. He was sweating. He really believed this marble had magic in it, for he had seen Mark shoot twenty out of twenty. And Mark was only a fair marble player. But he knew he was terrible at marbles! He had accepted the offer to shoot in the exhibition because he loved the idea of having the whole school watch him. But he hadn't really thought about the fact that they would be watching him shoot marbles!

Leroy knelt down with his eyes on the marbles in the ring. The crowd was silent. He set Shiner between the thumb and the forefinger of his right hand. He looked up at the crowd. All eyes were on him.

He looked back at the ring. The marbles scattered around the circle looked terribly far away. He glanced up at the crowd again and then back at the marbles.

Sweat ran into his eyes and he wiped it away with his sleeve. He just couldn't stand the pressure! He closed his eyes and fired.

Leroy heard a sharp "plik."

His eyes popped open. A marble was lying outside the circle, and Shiner was nestled in the dirt inside! A broad grin

spread across Leroy's face. He picked up Shiner and fired again
– with his eyes open this time. Another marble flew from the
ring. He fired again and again.

Eighteen, nineteen, twenty!

The crowd cheered, much louder this time. Leroy stood
with sweat dripping off his chin, grinning before the audience
and basking in the applause.

"If Leroy can hit twenty with that marble," yelled a fifth-
grade boy, "it's got to be supernatural!"

Everyone laughed and there was more applause. Leroy's
face turned red, but the sound of the applause more than made
up for the embarrassment. He grinned broadly again.

As the applause died down, Ned Shipley, the red-headed
fourth-grader, cupped his hands around his mouth and yelled,
"It doesn't take anybody special to hit twenty with that marble!"

Mrs. Woods saw Mark's face turn red. "Let's have a hand
for our shooters!" she called. Everyone clapped and cheered.

"Now," she said, "the exhibition is over. You still have
fifteen minutes to play before the bell rings. Leroy, gather up
the marbles for me."

While the other children ran off to play, Leroy took Shiner
back to Mark. "Thanks," he said, handing the marble to Mark.
Mark put Shiner back into his pocket while Leroy ran to gather
up the marbles for Mrs. Woods.

Mark walked away with his head down, hands rammed
down into his pockets. Mrs. Woods watched him out of the
corner of her eye for the rest of recess. Mark stayed apart from
the others, looking gloomy. His mother couldn't tell if he was
discouraged, angry or both.

For Mark, the afternoon classes seemed to drag. He did his
work, but he felt miserable. At the first of math Mrs. Woods
called on him and he answered correctly, but he didn't look up

at her. Halfway through math class something happened that lifted his spirits for awhile. Ned Shipley had been showing off in class. His father taught eighth-grade math and he had obviously helped Ned with his homework. Ned raised his hand to answer every question, waving it energetically to get Mrs. Woods' attention.

Jamming his left hand into his pants pocket and clutching Shiner, Mark slumped down in his seat. Ned had just answered another difficult problem. The grin on Ned's face told everyone just how great Ned thought he was!

What a showoff, thought Mark in disgust. "I wish he had ants in his pants!" Mark muttered angrily under his breath. He was thinking of big red ants. Scowling, he looked back at his math book.

Moments later, a movement to the left of him caught his eye. He looked up. Ned was squirming in his seat. Mrs. Woods was looking at the next problem in her math book and did not notice.

Ned's squirm rapidly became a panic. He began slapping his thighs. "Ow!" he yelled. "Ow! Ow!"

Mrs. Woods looked up just as Ned jumped out of his seat and began dancing up and down, hollering and slapping at his legs furiously. He looked hilarious, and the children began laughing.

"What on earth is going on, Ned?" asked Mrs. Woods.

"Ow! I don't know! Ouch!" cried Ned. "Something—ow! Something is biting me! Ouch! May I be excused?"

"Certainly!" said Mrs. Woods

Ned ran for the door, slapping as he went. The laughter died down when the children looked back at Mrs. Woods. Mark stopped laughing, too, and then looked down. But his eyes caught a glimpse of the floor under Ned's desk. Eight or ten large red ants lay crushed on the floor!

Mark's eyes widened in amazement! He stared at his math book, but his mind was going a hundred miles an hour. How did those red ants get there?

Mrs. Woods asked him a math problem, and he answered her, again without looking up. Soon the miserable feeling returned, and he forgot about the ants.

They were already into geography by the time Ned came back into the room. When the last bell rang, Mark started to file out of the classroom with the other children, but Mrs. Woods called him back.

He walked to her desk and stood looking down at the floor.

"Mark," she asked gently, "what is going on in your mind and heart?"

"Oh, nothing," he mumbled.

"Mark, it's obvious that something is wrong. You and I love each other. We care about each other. And," she reminded him, "we're honest with each other."

Mark looked up at her. She could see hurt and anger in his tear-filled eyes. "I felt special because the marble came to me. And I felt special because I could beat anybody with Shiner! Even Billy Wilder!"

"When did you start feeling different, darling?" she asked quietly.

"At that stupid old exhibition!" he declared hotly. "I felt real good when I shot Shiner. But then Billy Wilder did just as good as me. And Leroy did as good as me. Then, when Ned Shipley said what he did, I just about died!"

He paused for a moment, and then went on, angry tears running down his cheeks. "I'm not as smart as Ned Shipley, and I can't run as fast as Billy Wilder. But I finally did something better than everybody else – and I really felt special.

At least 'til that stupid old exhibition. Now I'm ordinary again!" His eyes dropped.

Mother was silent for a moment, then she spoke. "Mark, I'm going to tell you something that may be hard to understand, but I'd like you to try."

He looked up. "Okay," he said, but with anger still in his eyes.

"Honey," she said, "we set up the exhibition to let all the children see the marble at the same time so we could stop all the whispering and note-passing in classes. They settled down after we announced the exhibition.

"I had no intention of hurting you, Mark," she continued. "I am sorry for the way Ned acted. But I think there is something out of all this that you need to learn."

"What?" asked Mark.

"I think you need to learn that having a supernatural marble doesn't make one person better than another."

"What do you mean, Momma?"

"Last night when you told me about beating Billy Wilder at marbles, I saw a new kind of look in your eye. This morning at recess I saw the same kind of look, only worse. Then at lunch as you left the room, the same look was there – but again it was worse."

"What look was it, Momma?"

"It was a look that said, 'I am really something! I am better than you people!' It was the wrong kind of pride, Mark," she said. "You were becoming proud because you had that marble. You were feeling that it made you better than the other children.

"Mark," Momma continued, "I want you to be proud in the right way and for the right reasons. It's okay to be glad you have Shiner. But it is not okay to feel that having Shiner makes you better than other people.

"Honey, I want you to grow up to be proud of the right things," she said, tears in her eyes. "I want you to be honest and to be proud because you are honest.

"I want you to be kind and be glad because you are kind. I want you to be a man who stands up for what he believes in, like your father was. And I want you to be proud you are that kind of man.

"But Mark," she stressed, "you've got to learn that it's not the things a person has that make him great. It's who he is inside."

Mark stood sullenly before her, eyes fixed on the floor.

"You can go on home now." Mother said. "I know you want to play with friends on the way. It's okay if you do. Just be home by five o'clock. I'll have supper ready."

She paused for a moment, "I love you, Mark."

He turned, still looking at the floor, and started out.

"Mark," she called after him, "pray for wisdom on this."

He left. Mrs. Woods sat for another five minutes praying.

While Mother prayed, a small figure crept from beneath the open window of her room into the bushes at the edge of the school yard. From the bushes, a pair of dark eyes watched Mark walk through the school yard and take the dirt road toward home.

# The Chest of Gold

ARK TRUDGED along, head down, occasionally kicking rocks and sticks in the dusty road. Mother would work a few more minutes at the school and then start for home.

Without stopping to play with the other kids, he hurried to reach the turn-off to the river road before Mother caught up with him. He needed time alone to think.

He pushed his brown hair out of his eyes. "If only it were curly, like Allan Barnes'," he thought. All the girls liked Allan's curly blond hair and green eyes. But Mark's hair was straight and his eyes were just ordinary brown.

Mark wished he were the tallest boy in class. But three of the girls were even taller than he. And several of the boys were heavier built and had bigger muscles. "I'm not even the smallest," thought Mark wryly, "I'm just average."

His thoughts were suddenly interrupted.

"Lucky boy!" a voice called out. "Lucky boy! Come over here!"

Mark looked up. He had just rounded a sharp curve in the road. About fifty feet ahead, under a large oak tree by the right side of the road, stood a curious figure dressed in green.

Mark thought at first the person was a child, but the voice, though higher-pitched than an adult's, seemed too old for a child. As he drew closer Mark thought perhaps the person was a small man.

"Over here, lucky boy!" The figure waved for him to come.

The little man's voice had a slight metallic ring to it.

Mark hurried to the opposite side of the road. "My mother doesn't allow me to talk to strangers. Goodbye!" he blurted.

Mark walked even faster, watching the figure from the corner of his eye, ready to run if needed. The figure stopped gesturing. Mark could see that he wasn't a child, nor was he just a small man – at least not like any man Mark had ever seen. He was slightly taller than Mark and thin. He had straight black hair and was dressed in green trousers and a loose green shirt, both trimmed in black.

"I know where your marble came from and am prepared to buy it from you at a handsome price. See!" the person called.

Mark looked back. The little man held up a small, dark wooden box with a lid on it. It reminded Mark of the jewelry chest which sat on Mother's dresser.

The little man stepped from beneath the shade of the great oak into the sunlight and raised the lid of the chest. Large, shiny golden coins gleamed inside! The little box was brimming with them!

The flash of gold stopped Mark in his tracks. He turned

around. "Tell me about the marble," he said cautiously.

"The marble you have is the Stone of Rangilor," said the little man. "It came to you suddenly yesterday afternoon. I am not sure exactly where you found it, but it entered your world at high speed."

"What's Rangilor?" asked Mark. "And what's the 'Stone of Rangilor'?"

"Rangilor was a good king of my land," explained the little man. "He made the Stone as a gift to his eldest son – me. By the power he had, he blessed the Stone so that it now has certain powers. You have seen some of them as you have played marbles.

"By the way," added the little man, "I saw the exhibition this afternoon. I thought it was terrible the way you were embarrassed and humiliated."

The little man's sympathy was like gasoline poured on a dying fire. Anger began to rise within Mark again, and his face grew red.

"But anyway," the little man continued, "the Stone was in my possession yesterday when an enemy desiring its power tried to take the Stone from me.

"Before he could get it I threw the Stone, and it passed through an opening between your world and mine. That is why it entered your world at high speed."

"Where is your world? I mean, aren't you from this world?" asked Mark in amazement.

"That would take too long to explain," answered the little man, "and I haven't much time. But here, come see the rest of my payment for the Stone. Come on over! Come look!"

He stepped back under the tree and stood beside a large, dark chest that Mark had not noticed before. The chest was heavily carved and looked ancient. Its curved lid came up to the little man's waist.

The little man threw back the lid and the bright color of gold dazzled Mark's eyes. The small chest of coins the little man had used to get his attention was nothing compared to the thousands of golden coins in this box!

Mark walked over to the large chest. Its wood gave off a pungent scent which smelled a lot like pine. Picking up a golden coin bigger than a quarter, the little man handed it to Mark. It felt quite heavy.

"Real gold is very heavy and quite soft," said the little man, smiling. "Bite into it and see."

Mark bit into it. The metal gave way slightly under the pressure of his teeth. "It must be almost solid gold!" he exclaimed.

"It *is* solid gold," confirmed the little man, still smiling.

"The Stone of Rangilor was mine. When it entered your world and you found it, it became yours." said the little man. "I am now prepared to buy it back from you. I will give you the gold in the small chest and also the gold in the large chest for the Stone."

"That's a lot of money," exclaimed Mark. How much he wasn't sure, but he knew it was a fortune. He and Mother would be rich! Mark's mind raced to think of all they could do with the money.

The little man seemed to read his mind. "Think of it," he said sympathetically, "the end of humiliation you went through today. I saw you ashamed before the crowd as that nobody, Leroy Grimes, used the Stone belonging to you. And I saw how it hurt you."

The hurt and anger began to build inside Mark again.

"With this gold you can go where you want, buy what you want, be what you want," said the little man. "You could buy your mother a car, a new house, and even furs. You could buy the whole town if you wanted!

"And then," he continued, "when you rode through town, people would watch you in envy. The money would be yours alone. No Billy Wilder or Leroy Grimes would share your honor or shame you."

The anger welled up inside Mark as he remembered how the crowd had cheered for Leroy.

"Give me your supernatural marble," offered the little man, pointing toward the gold, "and all this is yours." Then he held out his hand, smiling.

Mark's anger had been seething and almost ready to erupt into full-scale revenge until he heard the word "supernatural." Something about the word bothered him. It jogged his memory. Mark stuck his hand in his pocket and clutched Shiner.

The little man noticed the change in Mark's expression. "Is there something wrong?" he asked nervously.

"No, no," said Mark in a distant voice. There seemed to be something extremely important he needed to remember, but he couldn't think of it. He closed his eyes and tried to concentrate.

Then he remembered! Dr. Taylor had said if the marble was supernatural, he would need to pray for wisdom, keep a pure heart, and double-check his facts.

Mark prayed silently and quickly for wisdom. He saw that his heart wasn't pure. Momma was right – he had been proud. And he had really been feeling sorry for himself. Momma would call it "self pity." And he had even been mad enough at Billy and Leroy and Momma to want to get back at them. Mark admitted he had been wrong to let those things pile up in his heart, and inside himself, decided to stop.

"Are you feeling all right?" asked the little man.

Mark's thinking began to clear. Now he needed to double-check the facts. Mark decided to ask the little man some questions.

"What is your name?" he asked.

The little man squirmed.

"This is not necessary," he hedged. "We have a financial matter to transact, and then I must be off. I am in a great hurry."

"Tell me your name," Mark demanded.

The little man squirmed more, looking like he was struggling against something. "Badrin of Rinsil-Don," he gasped, and then quickly regained his composure.

"See here," the little man said testily. "Will you sell me the Stone or not?"

"Is the Stone really yours?" questioned Mark.

"Of course not!" retorted the little man quickly. "It is now yours. But when I buy it from you it will be mine – again." He added the last word hastily.

Something still did not seem right to Mark. He prayed again for wisdom.

"Sell me the Stone so I can be on my way. The opening between your world and mine will close soon, and it will take me days to find another!"

An idea clicked in Mark's mind. "Look me in the eyes!" he ordered. Although Badrin obviously did not want to, he turned his eyes toward Mark. He reminded Mark of Leroy, fidgeting during Mrs. Woods' questioning.

"Tell me the truth. Did the Stone really belong to you?"

A violent shudder ran through Badrin's body. "No!" he said in a choking voice.

"Then I'm not going to sell it to you," declared Mark.

"Then I will take it!" shrieked the little man. He pounced on Mark, knocking him to the ground. They rolled over and over in the dust. Badrin's fingers gripped Mark's arms like the jaws of pliers! As they wrestled, the little man wrapped his arms around Mark. His strength was incredible! Mark struggled to breathe as Badrin's arms tightened like a vise.

"Give me the Stone or I will crush you!" Badrin shouted. He rolled over on top of Mark.

"You will not!" Mark yelled back, clutching Shiner even more tightly.

Then several things happened at once. Badrin's arms, legs and body went rigid. He fell off of Mark and lay on his back, his whole body stiff.

"Ahhhh! How did you know?" yelled the little man. "How did you know?"

Mark got up and backed away from the little man lying paralyzed and screaming on the ground.

At that moment Mark heard Mrs. Woods voice around the curve of the road. "Mark! Mark! Are you okay? Mark! What's happening?"

Mark could hear her running. He turned and ran toward her. She met him in the middle of the curve. Throwing his arms around her waist, he hugged her tightly and began to cry.

"The man!" he sobbed. "The man!" With one arm Mark pointed back down the road.

Mother quickly stepped to the side of the road. She broke a large branch from a dead tree limb lying in the tall grass. It made a fine club.

"Where is the man, honey?" she asked.

"Just around the curve," Mark gasped. But when they looked, no one was there! Mark looked at the tree. The chest of gold was gone! He was so surprised that he stopped crying. He ran to the great oak tree.

"Not too close to the bushes, Mark," Mother warned, "in

case he is still here."

"Come look, Momma!" Mark called.

Mother cautiously approached the tree, club poised and ready.

"See, Momma! He had a big chest of solid gold coins sitting here." Mark pointed to the deep rectangular impression left in the sparse grass.

A golden glint caught Mark's eye. He picked up a gold coin lying in a patch of grass. The coin had teeth prints in it. Mark handed it to Mother.

Suddenly Mark realized how strong the little man must be if he could lift the chest full of gold and run away with it. Then Mark thought of what Badrin could have done to him! He shivered.

"Are you okay, Mark?" asked Mother anxiously.

"I just have a few scratches. But Momma, this has been the strangest thing yet."

"Tell me about it on the way home, darling," said Mother. "Let's not stay here any longer!"

As they walked the rest of the way home, Mark told her the whole story.

"Well," she said when he had finished, "I think we'd better talk this incident over with Dr. Taylor. I think I see some things myself, but I'd sure like his opinion."

When they reached the house, Mother went inside to phone Dr. Taylor. Mark walked around back to find Trace. The big black pup was lying with his head on his paws and his long, black body stretched out behind him.

When he saw Mark, Trace lept to his feet with a bark of joy. He raced over to Mark, jumping and running in circles, and then rolled over on his back. Laughing, Mark bent down and scratched Trace's stomach.

"Hello, boy. Did you miss me? You wouldn't believe what's happened today," Mark said. Picking up a stick, he threw it hard, and Trace bounded to get it. They played fetch for a while.

When Mark went inside, Mother was setting out the ingredients for dinner. She told him to start a fire in the cookstove. Dr. Taylor and his mother would be coming over for dinner. Mother seemed pleased that they could come. So was Mark, for he liked them both. Mrs. Taylor always asked him about school. And she liked Trace.

While he worked to build the fire, Mark thought about Dr. Taylor. Although his hair was mostly gray, he sure didn't act or seem old. And he really knew how to throw a baseball. When the men played ball Dr. Taylor was always one of the pitchers.

Mark shook the cold ashes from the fire compartment and shoveled them into the bucket beside the stove. Next, he wadded up paper and put it inside the compartment. Then he carefully placed some kindling on top of the paper. Once it caught fire, Mark would add other chunks of wood.

Mark had a thought. Turning around, he asked his mother, "Do you think you will ever marry Dr. Taylor?"

Her face turned bright red! "Why, Mark!" she said, "What an awkward question!"

"But do you think you would?" pressed Mark as he turned to get a match from the box on the wall, next to the stove. "I really like him. I think he would make a great dad. And you are already a great mother, and you are very pretty . . . . After all, its been more than two years since his wife died."

"Mark, really!" protested his mother. Her face was still crimson when he turned around again.

"Well?" he asked.

"He is a fine man and would make a fine father," said Mother, "but he is thirteen years older than I am!"

"But, he can still really play baseball," replied Mark, "And he's big and strong. Don't you think he's handsome? And doesn't he make enough money to support a family?"

Mother laughed. "Yes, Dr. Taylor is a handsome man, and a good baseball player, and he earns enough money to support a family. But choosing a husband is the mother's decision, not the son's. And the son needs to get the fire going!"

## In Outer Space

"MADELYN, the whole dinner was delicious, but the chocolate pie was wonderful!" said Dr. Taylor as he placed his fork on his now-empty plate.

Mark watched Mrs. Taylor pat her mouth with her napkin. To Mark her silver hair and kind face with its deep lines made her look just like a grandmother ought to look.

"It's a wonder that a good cook like you hasn't married again," teased Mrs. Taylor with a twinkle in her eye.

Mark looked at Mother with a slight smile, and her face turned red.

"I guess the right man and the right time haven't come together for me," said Mother, attempting a cheery smile.

"I think Momma would make a great wife for somebody," put in Mark. "She's already a great mother."

"Well, I will put out the news about how good a cook your mother is," promised Mrs. Taylor with a wink at Mark. "Maybe I could help the right man and the right time come together faster."

Mark grinned at Mrs. Taylor and nodded his head slightly toward the doctor who was finishing his coffee. Mrs. Taylor smiled back at Mark and winked again.

Mother looked down at the table, pretending she had not seen the exchange of signals. "Mark, help me clear the table, please," she asked.

Mark just then realized that his own plate was still two-thirds full. He had done most of the talking: telling the story of the marble's appearance, the game at church last night, the exhibition at afternoon recess, and his experience with the little man on the way home from school. Then Mother had shown them the gold coin.

"Yes, Mother. But may I keep my plate and finish eating?"

"Certainly, dear," answered Mother. She poured the doctor another cup of coffee. Then she and Mark cleared most of the dishes from the table and sat down again. Dr. Taylor took a sip of coffee, patted his mouth with his napkin and pushed his chair back slightly from the table.

"What do you think, Jim?" Mother asked.

The doctor thought for a moment. "Several things come to mind," he said. "First, it definitely appears that we are dealing with both the supernatural – and another world. A stone that has power like Mark's marble and a little man who could run while carrying a chest of gold – neither are normal occurrences in our world.

"What do you think we should do?" asked Mrs. Woods.

"The advice I gave you seems to be working. I would encourage you to keep on with it. Pray for wisdom, keep a pure heart and double-check your facts."

"A second thing," Dr. Taylor continued, "since this Badrin character lied about owning the Stone, he may have lied about other things. He could be a confused person trying to lie for a good reason. But it sounds like he's mixed up with the Father of Lies. My guess is that he is evil and means evil.

"Third, Badrin wants the Stone, so he'll probably be back.

"Fourth, I think Badrin made a mistake when he asked how you knew, Mark," said the doctor.

"What do you mean Dr. Taylor?" asked Mark. "I don't know why Badrin said that!"

"When you asked Badrin questions, he either avoided your questions or he lied to you," said the doctor.

"That's right," said Mark.

"But when you demanded that he tell you his name, when you told him to tell the truth, and when you commanded him not to crush you, he had to obey you," reasoned the doctor.

"Yes, sir. But when he said he would crush me, I didn't really command him not to; I just told him he wasn't going to."

"And that," said Mother, "was like a command."

"I guess I didn't think about it like that."

"What Badrin probably was asking you, Mark, was how did you know that you had power to command him," suggested the doctor.

"Gosh!" Mark exclaimed. "You mean I have the power to make him do what I want?"

"You at least have the power to make him speak," answered Dr. Taylor, "to make him speak the truth, and to paralyze him."

"But why? How did I get it?" wondered Mark.

"Well, one possibility," said the doctor, "is that people of our world have power over people from Badrin's world when they come into ours. But I think it's probably something else."

"The Stone!" cried Mother. "The Stone of Rangilor! Perhaps that's one of it's powers!"

"That's my guess, too, Madelyn," said the doctor. "It could be that the Stone gives the one who has it the power to control Badrin – or even others."

"Really?" asked Mark, his eyes wide. Then he remembered the red ants on the floor of the classroom!

"Something else happened at school," Mark confessed, looking at his plate. He told how he had wished for red ants in Ned Shipley's pants – and what happened. He thought Mother would be angry, but she just sat there, looking at him in amazement.

"Well, that fits the pattern," said Dr. Taylor. "You have a marble in your possession that has powers at which we can only guess. But you need to be careful what you do with it, Mark. What happened to Ned was an accident, but you could easily kill someone in just such an accident! What if you had wished Ned Shipley were dead?"

Mark sat in silence, staggered by the thought.

"What do you think is going to happen, Jim?" asked Mother. Mark could see the worry in her face.

"I'm no prophet, Madelyn," the doctor sighed, "but I'd be surprised if Badrin didn't try to get the Stone again. You may run into other unusual persons involved with this Stone as well.

"One thing's for sure," he said, his kind, blue eyes looking steadily into Mark's. "You're going to learn a whole lot in a short time, Mark."

Mother and the Taylors chatted for a few more minutes. But Mark didn't really hear what they were saying. His mind was reeling. Power over Badrin? Over others? Power from the Stone? Wherever the power came from, it was his. If that

Badrin showed up again, he'd show him a thing or two! A smirk began to spread over Mark's face.

"Mark," said the doctor. Mark looked up at him. The doctor's eyes showed concern. "I don't want to be harsh with you, son, but if the pride that shows on your face is in your heart, you are headed for trouble. If you become proud, your enemy will easily trap you."

"Yes, sir," replied Mark, dropping his eyes. He didn't want to become prideful. He was old enough to know that after people became proud they usually did something stupid.

"Jim, should we hide the Stone, destroy it, give it away, or do something else with it?" worried Mother.

"I think it would be best to keep it until the rightful owner appears. If it is as powerful as it seems, the right people should be after it before too long. And it would be handy to have the Stone if Badrin or others like him show up.

"Mark will be their likely target," he continued. "It would be just as well if he kept the Stone with him. Only be careful, Mark, and don't be playing with it," he warned. "You don't know its power for good or evil, so you don't want to lose it and have it fall into the wrong hands!"

"I don't think a kid in town would play marbles with me anyway if I used Shiner," laughed Mark.

Dr. Taylor looked at his watch and said that they needed to be going. Mother and Mark walked the Taylors out onto the porch.

"I will be driving to Riverport tonight," said Dr. Taylor. "All day tomorrow I will be in meetings with the regional Medical Association. It will be rather difficult to get in touch with me by phone. But I should be back here in Radford by Saturday afternoon. When I arrive home I will call to see how things are going."

Dr. Taylor helped his mother down the steps and into his car.

"Oh, I almost forgot!" said the doctor, turning and walking back to the porch. "These are for you, Mark," he smiled as he took two peppermints out of his coat pocket.

"Thank you, sir!" grinned Mark.

"See you Saturday!" called the doctor as he walked back to his car. Mark and Mother waved them off and then walked back into the house. They were finishing up the dishes when a knock came at the front door.

Randy Starnes, Mark's best friend, was standing on the porch. He asked if Mark could play for a few minutes. Since Mark had finished all his homework at school, Mother said it would be okay – if they stayed close to the house. She would finish cleaning the kitchen and then grade papers while they played. She also quietly reminded Mark not to mention Badrin and the events of the day.

Mark and Randy went outside and stood at the edge of the porch, trying to decide what to play. Twilight was fading, and the night promised to be a beautiful one. The stars coming out sparkled like diamonds in the darkening sky. A faint yellow glow on the horizon signalled the moon would be up before long.

Sounds of the night began to fill the air. Crickets began to sing. From across the road, a whippoorwill added his song to the crickets'. The damp smell of the cool evening air enveloped the boys. It was an evening just made for adventure!

Since the stars were so bright and crisp, the boys decided to play "Invaders from Beyond." Both boys had seen the movie the previous Saturday at the small theater in town. And both wanted to be Commander Colt, the hero of the movie. So, they struck a compromise: Randy would play Commander Colt first and then Mark would.

Two rocking chairs always sat on the porch. The boys pulled them over to the edge of the porch so that they could see the stars well. The wide wooden arms and hard wooden bottoms already felt damp from the cool, moist air, but they made excellent spaceship seats. Climbing into the chairs, the boys rocketed off into space.

Randy led them in a battle against the spaceships of the evil space emperor, a battle that involved a good deal of jumping off the porch and rolling around on the ground in hand-to-hand combat.

Next, came Mark's turn. He decided that their next adventure would be on the moon. The moon was just peeking above the horizon and looked like an enormous orange ball.

Sitting in his rocker, Mark held his left hand as though it grasped the steering wheel on Commander Colt's spaceship. With his right hand he dug a marble out of his pocket and held it tightly. It would be the knob on the spaceship's accelerator stick.

Focusing intently on the rising moon he called out, "Next stop, the moon." He pulled back on the imaginary steering wheel and thrust the "accelerator stick" forward.

He and Randy began talking excitedly back and forth about the spaceship and planning what they would do to the evil people who had invaded the moon.

Mark was having a great time! The stars were zipping by and the moon was looking larger when Mark noticed that Randy had been silent for a moment.

"Mark?" Randy asked in a weak, wavering voice. "Mark?"

"Commander Colt," corrected Mark, caught up in the play.

"Mark, we're not on the porch," quavered Randy with

panic in his voice.

"Commander Co – !" Mark turned to look at Randy and stopped in mid-sentence. His eyes widened in shock!

Randy was dressed in a gray, one-piece space suit, just like the one Commander Colt had worn in the movie. He was sitting in a large, gray leather spaceship chair with a seatbelt buckled around him. The gray walls of a spaceship curved behind him and up over his head. Randy's eyes bulged with fear. He was still in control himself – but just barely!

Mark's eyes quickly followed the curve of the ship's ceiling on over his own head. He saw, in place of the hard rocker, a soft, gray leather chair. He, too, had on a snug-fitting space suit and seatbelt!

"Oh, no!" gasped Mark, his face going white. He turned and looked forward. Through a huge, clear windshield the moon was growing larger. Beneath the windshield was an instrument panel full of gauges and red, yellow and green lights.

The fingers of Mark's left hand were wrapped around a steering wheel that felt like steel. His right hand rested on top of a stick protruding from the panel in front of him.

The air smelled much like the inside of Dr. Taylor's Buick. From behind them came a low roar of a powerful engine.

"It can't be!" whispered Mark.

"We're in outer space!" Randy yelled.

## The Night Visitor

ARK STARED through the windshield as though
in a trance. The moon rapidly grew larger until
it filled their entire view.

"I can see mountains and valleys," said
Randy slowly. He had calmed down consid-
erably. Mark made no comment.

"We're going down awfully fast, Mark," Randy noticed
anxiously. "And we're heading right toward those mountains."
The spaceship plunged ahead, and the mountains swiftly filled
their view. One mountain loomed larger and larger in front of
them. Randy panicked.

"Mark!" he screamed. "Mark! Do something!"

Mark snapped out of his trance. He remembered seeing
Commander Colt avoid a crash just like this in the movie.
Grabbing the steering wheel with both hands, he wrenched it to

the left and pulled back hard! The ship instantly turned left and the nose lifted. But still the right wing brushed an outcrop of rocks!

The ship veered wildly! Mark and Randy were slammed around in their seats, but Mark held on tightly to the wheel. The ship stabilized and climbed swiftly, banking steeply to the left. The force of the turn and climb drove them deep into their seats. Mark felt as though he weighed a thousand pounds, with each of his arms weighing at least a hundred! Even his jaws sagged.

Then Mark remembered the accelerator! He dropped his arm to the accelerator stick and pulled back. The speed of their climb slowed and the force weighing them down lightened. Mark put both hands back on the wheel, straightened it out and pushed forward, leveling the ship. He leaned forward in his seat. Below them huge peaks were zipping past as they flew along a range of great mountains.

Mark again pulled back on the accelerator, further reducing their speed. When he took his hand off the knob he saw Shiner mounted firmly on the top of the accelerator stick!

"The Stone!" said Mark wide-eyed. He looked back at the windshield. Ahead of the ship Mark could see a few more peaks and then a vast, flat plain, pock-marked with craters.

"What happened?" asked Randy, his voice still shaky. "H-H-How did we get here?"

"I think it has something to do with Shiner," answered Mark, concentrating on guiding the ship. "You know, my supernatural marble."

They were coming to the last mountain peak before the plain. Suddenly, a bright, red beam of light streaked across the nose of the spaceship and hit the peak on their left. The top of the mountain exploded! Red, molten lava spewed from the jagged peak and poured down the sides of the mountain!

"What was that?" exclaimed Randy.

Another streak of red light flashed across the ship's nose, hitting the plain in a blinding explosion. The beam had come from above and behind them.

"I hope it's not what I think it is!" said Mark. He pulled up the nose of the spacecraft and they shot up from the moon's surface. Mark banked the spaceship in a sharp left turn and then righted the ship. A moment later they spied two flat, red and black bat-winged spaceships bearing down on them, firing red streaks of light.

"Oh no!" moaned Randy. "Moon invaders!"

"Just like in the movie!" exclaimed Mark.

In the movie the firing button for the guns on Commander Colt's spacecraft had been to the right of the accelerator. Mark glanced to the right and saw a big red button with the words "LIGHT CANNON" beneath it. He pressed the button, and a beam of blue light shot out from the nose of their ship, narrowly missing one of the invaders!

Both enemy ships fired at once. The boys felt a violent shock. They heard an explosion inside the ship behind them. Their spacecraft started shuddering.

"We're hit!" yelled Randy. Pressing the red button again, Mark returned their fire but missed. Then their ship suddenly jerked to the right and swiftly plunged toward the surface. Mark frantically turned the wheel left and right.

"I can't control it!" he yelled, "We're going to crash!"

"I don't want do die out here!" cried Randy hysterically. "I want to go home!"

"So do I, but I don't know how!" yelled Mark, pulling back on the wheel and the accelerator knob.

Suddenly, the moon and the batwing spacecraft were gone. And the windshield itself was gone! Mark found himself staring at a night sky. He felt a hard seat beneath him and knew he was sitting in the rocking chair on the front porch! Around him the crickets were singing.

He looked over at Randy, swaying back and forth in the rocker next to him, eyes wide. The full yellow moon had risen completely, and the bright moonlight was rapidly replacing the glitter of the stars.

With a huge sigh Randy collapsed back into the rocker. He just sat there, staring at nothing. Neither he nor Mark spoke for several minutes. Finally Mark asked, "Do you think we were really out in space and flying over the moon? Or did we just imagine it?"

"I don't know," answered Randy. "But I don't ever want to do that again! The next time we play something, you leave your supernatural marble at home!"

"I will," Mark nodded vigorously. "I thought we were going to die up there!"

"Mark?" called Mother from inside the house. "Time for bed!"

"I've got to go home, too." said Randy, rising to leave. "But I don't know if I'll be able to sleep after this!" Before he jumped off the porch, he turned, "Oh yes, I'm not going to say anything about this to my mother. If I tell her she'll whip me for lying!"

"Okay," agreed Mark.

After Randy left, Mark went inside to get ready for bed. Mother came into his room as he was crawling under the covers.

"Boy, this stuff is really strange, Momma," declared Mark as she sat down on the edge of his bed. He told her all about the space adventure.

Trying to remain calm, Mother asked him several questions about the space trip. Then she extracted a promise from Mark not to take any more fantasy trips.

"You're right, Mark," she said. "This incident is really strange, but I have felt strange about all that's happened since the marble first appeared. I don't quite know what to think. I guess I'm excited and afraid at the same time."

"That's how I feel," agreed Mark, "excited and scared."

Mother sat silent for a moment, lost in thought.

"Mother, could I have Trace sleep in my room tonight?" asked Mark. "He could be a guard dog."

"I think it would be okay, Honey. We'll let him stay tonight, but we won't make a practice of it. Do you want to go and get him?"

Mark jumped out of bed and ran downstairs. Moments later he was back with the big pup bounding behind him. Mark climbed into bed while Trace padded over beside him, put his front paws on the covers and licked Mark's face. Then Mother pushed the pup's paws off the bed.

Trace just sat there, mouth open, tongue out, panting and smiling. But he gave no evidence he intended to lie down.

"I'll turn the light out in your room and leave the hall light on," promised Mother, rising from the bed. She bent over and kissed him on the forehead. "There's a goodnight kiss from someone who loves you very much. Let's pray together and then get some sleep."

So Mark and Mother prayed for protection. Then she turned out the light, leaving the bedroom door open slightly so the light from the hall would shine faintly into his room.

A few hours later a noise roused Mark from sleep. He thought he heard Trace growling. Rolling over, he raised up on his elbow and rubbed his eyes sleepily.

"What's the matter, Trace?" he mumbled, slowly opening

his eyes. "What is it, boy?" In the faint light he saw Trace's black form backed under the nightstand beside his bed, flattened against the floor. All that Mark could make out clearly were his eyes and bared teeth. A low growl came from him.

Mark looked in the direction that Trace was growling. By the light from the hallway he thought he could see someone about his size sitting on his bed! Mark rubbed his eyes and looked a second time, trying to focus his sleepy eyes in the dim light.

There, sitting on the bed beside him was a little man. Mark's eyes popped wide open! The little man smiled broadly. "Hail, blessed of the Holy One!" he said in a cheerful voice with a slight metallic ring.

Mark screamed at the top of his lungs and dove under the bed covers. Trace began to bark wildly.

"Mark!" called Mother. "Mark, what's wrong?" Mark could hear her running down the hallway into his room. "It's me, Mark," she said. "It's Mother. It's okay. You can come out now."

Mark peeped cautiously out from under the covers. There was Mother sitting beside him in her long nightgown, her hair around her shoulders and her eyes full of concern. The light was on in his bedroom. She was pulling back the covers from Mark's face.

"Oh, Momma!" cried Mark, throwing his arms around her neck and hugging her tightly. He was shaking but not crying.

"What happened, Mark?" she asked anxiously.

"Trace was growling and woke me up. When I looked around, there was a little man sitting on my bed. I screamed and hid under the covers!"

"Was it Badrin?"

"Well," Mark paused, trying to recall. "I don't think so."

"What did he look like?" Mother asked.

"He had blond hair," said Mark. "Badrin's hair is black. But he was the same kind of person, not a child but not a man either. He was small and thin. I think he was wearing the same kind of clothes as Badrin.

"But I felt different about him than how I felt about Badrin," added Mark thoughtfully. "I didn't like Badrin, but I think I felt good about this person."

"Then why did you scream, Honey?" Mother asked.

"I don't know," said Mark. "I guess it happened so fast it scared me. Oh yes, the little man said, 'Hail, Blessed of the Holy One!'"

Mother got up and strode to the corner behind the door where Mark kept his baseball bat. Picking up the bat, she looked under the bed and in Mark's closet. She found no one.

"Stay behind me, and we'll check the rest of the house!"

Mark climbed out of bed. "C'mon, Trace!" he called. But Trace wouldn't come out from under the night stand. In fact, he was still growling softly. Mark tried pulling him out, but as soon as Mark got him out, Trace scooted back under the stand.

"Some guard dog!" snorted Mark in disgust.

"Even though he's big," said Mother, "he's still just a pup, and puppies scare easily. Leave him alone, and follow me."

With Mark behind her, Mother checked the guest bedroom, her bedroom, the bathroom, and the hall closet. Then they cautiously crept downstairs, turning on lights as they checked every room. Both the front and back doors were still locked with the keys in the latches inside the house. All the windows were still locked from the inside. They found no one.

"You'll sleep with me the rest of the night," decided Mother.

Mark breathed a sigh of relief. Even though he was almost

ten, he didn't want to spend the rest of the night alone, just in case another strange person appeared in his room. They stopped by Mark's room, and Mark tried to coax Trace to follow them. But Trace wouldn't budge.

In Mother's bedroom Mark climbed into the big four-poster bed and snuggled down under the covers. Mother leaned the baseball bat against her nightstand, left the light on and got into bed. In a short time Mother was asleep. But every time Mark closed his eyes for more than a minute he thought he felt someone sit down on his side of the bed. After a long time he fell asleep.

## Kintras of Stargis-Lin

HE NEXT MORNING Mark fetched Trace from his bedroom, took him outside and fed him. After breakfast, he and Mother set out for school. Normally Mark would have run ahead, but today they walked side by side, Mark carrying his baseball bat over his shoulder.

Mother told Mark to tell no one about Badrin or about the strange visitor in the night. But if anything unusual happened during the day, Mark was to let her know immediately.

The early morning passed quickly. At recess Mark looked for Randy. Randy was a grade ahead of Mark. Randy's teacher told Mark that Randy was absent, so Mark decided to walk by himself.

With his hands in his pockets and his head down, he slowly wandered over the school yard thinking about the events of last night. He didn't realize he was getting so close to a clump of bushes bordering the playground.

"Hail, Blessed of the Holy One!" called a voice from the bushes. The slight metallic ring to the voice caused Mark to freeze in his tracks.

Mark's head jerked up. About twenty feet in front of him, standing behind a sparse bush, stood a blond-haired little man dressed in green trousers and and an overshirt trimmed in gold. He was smiling. His face looked like a twenty-five-year-old's – except it had the look of authority.

Mark rammed his hand into his pocket and grasped Shiner.

"I command you to stand still!" Mark said forcefully, but not loud enough for the other children to hear.

"Though you have no power to command me, I shall stand still," calmly replied the little man. "I gather you have met Badrin of Rinsil-Don," he added with a trace of amusement.

For a moment Mark was bewildered. Should he run, scream, command or what? Then he remembered: first, pray for wisdom! He prayed quickly. Next, look for a pure heart; things seemed to be in order. And last, double-check the facts. He decided to ask questions.

"Tell me your name," demanded Mark.

"My name is Kintras of Stargis-Lin."

"Look me in the eye," Mark ordered. The little man obeyed. Mark noticed a faint scar that ran down the left side of the little man's face. "Tell me your true name," commanded Mark, hoping to catch him if he was lying. But the blue eyes of the little man were clear and steady.

"Kintras of Stargis-Lin," replied the little man as he struggled to hold back a smile.

"Tell me the truth about Badrin of Rinsil-Don!" Mark

said, continuing to look Kintras in the eye.

"In our world Badrin is a Twisted One," explained Kintras. "In your world you would call him a criminal, though it is a bit more complicated than that.

"Badrin is here to try to get the Stone of Rangilor which entered your world two days ago. He prefers to acquire the stone legally, but he will use whatever means he feels necessary, even violence, to obtain it."

"What is Rinsil-Don?"

"It is a city in our world, like Stargis-Lin." Kintras did not take his eyes off Mark, but he sat down.

"I command you to stand!" cried Mark, frightened by the movement.

"Mark," replied Kintras patiently, "you cannot command me as you do Badrin."

Mark stepped back a couple of paces, ready to run if needed. Obviously he couldn't control Kintras, for the little man remained seated.

But Kintras continued to look Mark in the eyes. "I will do you no harm," he assured Mark.

"How do I know that?" Mark asked.

"I am not a Twisted One," said Kintras. "I am a servant of the Holy One."

"How do I know?"

"Badrin would not be able to look you in the eye and speak," said Kintras, "but I can. Also, as you came near to Badrin, you would have felt dread. When near me, though you are cautious, you sense peace."

"Tell me about the Stone of Rangilor."

"Rangilor was a good king in our world. He made the Stone and gave it great power. At his death he entrusted it to his eldest son, me, to use for the benefit of our people.

"The Stone has many beneficial powers; it can find objects and do other things. But its greatest blessing is that it helps us greatly limit the powers of the Twisted Ones in our world.

"Badrin desires the Stone so he can become the greatest among the Twisted Ones and rule over them. He also wants to use it to destroy us."

"Do you mean that you are not from this world – I mean Earth?" asked Mark.

"No, I am not from your world," answered Kintras. "I am from the world of Tarlis."

Mark thought for a moment. "Tell me what a 'Twisted One' is," he said.

"It is complicated." said Kintras. "There is a difference between our worlds. The ones who began your world were extremely foolish, and as a result, all of you are 'broken.' On the inside, each of you is more or less a rebel. So even when you want to do right, you also want to do wrong. Though you may do right for a moment, it will not be long until you do wrong. You do not have the power to keep doing only good. You have some control over your criminals but not very much.

"Those who began our world also acted foolishly, but not so much as your ancestors," continued Kintras. "Most who live in our world continue to do right. We serve the Holy One.

"The Twisted Ones are the few people who have decided to do wrong, and they serve the Enemy. Our control over them is much greater than your control over the criminals in your world."

"How did the Stone get into my house?" asked Mark.

"Badrin persuaded one of the guards of the Stone to twist himself," said Kintras. "The guard stole the Stone and gave it to Badrin. We pursued Badrin to one of the borders between our world and yours. Just before we caught him, he threw the Stone of Rangilor through an opening into your world.

"We caught Badrin, but, with the help of the twisted guard, he escaped and entered your world."

The bell signaling the end of recess rang.

"I've got to go back inside now," said Mark, glancing back at the children filing into school. "But before I go, were you the one in my room last night?"

"Yes," replied Kintras.

"Why did you scare me?" asked Mark.

"It was my ignorance," said Kintras. "I know little of humans. My choices of timing and appearance were ill-judged, but I had no desire to frighten you.

"Mark," said Kintras earnestly, "I have come to ask you for the Stone of Rangilor. I want to talk further with you."

"Do you know where the turn-off from the main road to the river is?" asked Mark.

"Yes, I know the geography of your area."

"Good," said Mark. "meet me there after school."

"I will," promised Kintras. "And thank you."

Mark ran to class.

During lunch Mark told his mother all about the conversation with Kintras of Stargis-Lin.

"I agree, Mark, that it sounds like this Kintras is telling the truth," she said. "But all the same, I don't like the idea of you meeting him alone on the river road. I think I will go along with you."

Mark was glad, for he was nervous about going alone. The rest of the afternoon passed even slower than most Friday afternoons. Finally school was out. Setting out together, Mother carried her books and purse while Mark carried his baseball bat.

Wildflowers dotted both sides of the road, reaching above the new blades of spring grass. They reached the junction with the river road and stood in the shade of a large tree. Purple wildflowers blooming across the road gave off a pleasant fragrance. Mark watched as bees and yellow butterflies flitted among them.

But Kintras was not there.

A while later Mother looked at her wrist watch. "We've been standing here for fifteen minutes," she said. "I think I'll sit down." She spread her books on the ground in the shade of the tree and sat on them. Thirty minutes passed, then forty-five.

"I think we'd better go home, Mark," finally Mother said. "If Kintras were going to show, he would have been here by now."

"I guess you're right, Momma," sighed Mark, helping her up to her feet. "I just don't understand it. I thought he was really honest."

"Well, maybe he is. Maybe something went wrong. But then again . . . maybe he isn't. We'll just have to wait and see."

They walked home in silence. When they reached the house, Mother went inside to start supper, and Mark went to chop firewood for Saturday's breakfast.

As Mark was crossing the back yard to the barn, Trace came running around the corner of the barn. When he saw Mark he ran to him, barking. Mark patted his head. While Trace ran around the yard in circles, Mark walked to the barn.

He had just opened the barn door when, out of the corner of his eye, he saw Trace coming. Mark turned around, braced himself and spread his arms wide. Trace leaped right into them.

Mark caught him, laughing as he staggered backwards under the heavy load. He put his head against the side of Trace's head and hugged him tightly. Trace wriggled happily, and his coarse black fur scratched Mark's face.

Trace squirmed up and licked Mark's face vigorously.

Mark put Trace down. "We're not going to be able to do that much longer, Trace. Pretty soon you're going to be big enough to knock me down!"

Trace stood panting with his long, red tongue hanging out the side of his mouth. His switch-like tail whipped back and forth as Mark patted him on the head. Then he turned and ran for his water bucket near the porch.

While Trace took a long drink Mark got the axe from the barn. Walking around the edge of the barn farthest from the house, he headed toward the pile of small logs waiting to be split into stovewood.

Mark picked out a piece of wood and set it upright on the chopping block. He stepped back, and then swung the big axe with all his might. The head of the axe bit deeply into the brittle wood with a loud "thunk," splitting off a piece.

Bending over, Mark picked up the chunk and sniffed it. He loved the fresh, woody scent of the newly split pieces. Then pitching it aside, he set the log upright again. He took the axe and swung it back for another blow.

At that moment Trace came bounding around the corner of the barn, happy-go-lucky with his mouth wide open and tongue hanging out. Mark paused momentarily to warn him to stay back, but the dog came to a sliding halt, growling. The hair on the back of Trace's neck and shoulders stood up as he crouched down and started backing away.

Suddenly the piece of wood standing in front of Mark jumped several feet into the air! The wood hung suspended against the blue sky for a moment, and then crashed back to earth.

Trace let out a yelp and took off around the barn. Mark wasn't sure what was happening, but he wasn't going to stay around to find out! He dropped the axe and spun around to run back to the house.  But he found himself almost nose-to-nose with a little man!

# The Unseen Flaw

**ARK STARTED** to scream but then checked himself.

"Hail, Blessed of the Holy One!" the little man greeted him cheerfully.

"Kintras! You scared me!"

The little man looked puzzled. "I'm sorry, Mark," he apologized. "This is my first visit to your world, and I had much business to complete before I came. I studied only briefly about humans, and now I see I did not study enough. Twice I have misjudged. What I thought would be an interesting way to start a conversation has frightened you instead. I am sorry."

"It's okay," said Mark. "But why do you keep calling me 'Blessed of the Holy One'?"

"Because you are," replied Kintras simply.

"I don't understand. What is the 'Holy One'?"

Kintras looked surprised. "It is the name of the One whom I serve," he answered. "You do not know him?"

"Should I?" asked Mark.

"Again my preparation has been inadequate," said Kintras regretfully. He thought for a moment. "Do you know the word, 'God'?" he asked.

"Yes," replied Mark, puzzled. "I learn about Him at church. And my mother and I pray to Him at night."

"Good!" smiled Kintras. "He is the 'Holy One.' And you have been blessed by Him in many ways."

"Oh? What kinds of ways?" Mark wondered.

"One way is the mother you have," answered Kintras. "It is a blessing to have a mother who has loved you and taught you like she has."

"I know Momma is a good mother," agreed Mark. "But my father died when I was a baby. How can I be 'blessed' if that happened to me?"

"In your world many children do not have fathers," said Kintras, "but few have mothers like yours.

"You are also blessed because the Holy One has allowed you to possess the Stone of Rangilor."

"I don't see much blessing in that at all," snorted Mark. "It was fun at first, but now it's a bother – maybe even dangerous!"

"You have seen strange things happen by the power of the Stone," explained Kintras. "But you have been entrusted with something that is far more powerful than you realize. A great trust has been given to you. Put your hand in your pocket, grasp the Stone of Rangilor and command the wood pile to rise."

Mark stuck his hand into his pocket, held Shiner, and said, "I command the wood to rise!" Without any noises the whole great pile of wood slowly rose into the air until it was as high as Mark's head!

"Gosh!" whispered Mark in awe.

"Now, command it to lower," said Kintras.

"Lower to the ground," Mark commanded. The wood pile settled noiselessly to the ground.

"Wow!" exclaimed Mark. "I want to show Momma this!" He started to turn and run to the house.

"Please wait!" cried Kintras.

"Why?" asked Mark, halting abruptly.

"You may show her," said Kintras, "but first, I want to finish our conversation."

Suddenly Mark remembered that Kintras had not shown up at the river road. "Why didn't you show up at the river road?" Mark asked suspiciously.

"I did come," said Kintras.

"Well, I didn't see you," argued Mark.

"I saw you and your mother first stand, then sit, in the shade of the large tree on the south side of the road," replied Kintras. "And I stayed until I saw you help her up and the two of you start walking home."

"Then why didn't you come and talk to us?"

"It is forbidden for us to show ourselves undisguised to more than one person on a trip into your world. I cannot show myself undisguised to anyone but you."

"Why can't you show yourself to more than one person?" puzzled Mark.

"I do not know fully," answered Kintras thoughtfully. "I think it is to prevent your learned men from proving our existence. For then they would seek the doors into our world and spread your brokenness into it."

Kintras looked at the piece of firewood that had crashed back to the ground. "You were changing the size of this wood when I came. What size do you wish for your wood to become?"

"I have to split it so that each piece is about three inches thick. Why?" asked Mark.

"Picture wood of the proper size in your mind," answered Kintras. "Then hold the Stone in your hand and command all of the wood to split itself."

Mark pictured a piece of split firewood in his mind. Then he put his hand in his pocket and held Shiner. "Wood, split yourself!" he commanded.

A terrific groaning noise began. From somewhere around the barn Mark heard Trace start barking. Mark put his hands over his ears to block the sound. Then with a great, ear-shattering crack, the huge pile of wood jumped as it split into hundreds of firewood chunks! The pungent, woody scent of freshly cut wood tickled Mark's nose.

Mark removed his hands from his ears in time to hear Mother yelling, "Mark! Are you okay?"

He wheeled around just as she turned the corner of the barn. "Mark! What happened?" she gasped, out of breath. "I heard a terrible noise!"

"I split the firewood, Momma," he grinned.

Mother looked at the huge pile of split wood, and her mouth dropped open in amazement! "Mark! How on earth . . . ?"

"With Shiner. Kintras showed me how." He turned to point at Kintras but he wasn't there!

"Kintras was here?" Mother asked.

"Yes, Momma," said Mark. "But he left when you came." Mark then explained what Kintras had told him.

"Watch this!" he said, gripping Shiner in his pocket. "Wood rise," he commanded. Noiselessly the whole pile rose above the ground.

"My word!" gasped Momma.

"Wood, be lowered to the ground," commanded Mark. Just as silently the wood lowered until it rested on the ground.

"Oh, Mark!" Mother exclaimed. "This whole situation is even bigger than we thought! Who knows what damage Shiner could do in the hands of the wrong person!"

"Momma, I want to finish talking to Kintras," said Mark. "And he can't show himself to anyone but me."

"Then I'm afraid I'll have to leave you alone with him." Worry clouded her eyes for a moment, but then determination filled them. "Remember," she cautioned Mark, "pray for wisdom, keep a pure heart, and double-check your facts!"

She stooped down and hugged him close. "I love you, Honey," she whispered, her voice quivering. Mark looked up into her eyes. He could see tears swimming there. "I'll be praying."

Mark watched her walk around the corner of the barn. A few moments later he heard the back door bang shut.

"Hail, Blessed of the Holy One!" greeted a familiar voice.

Mark turned back around toward the wood pile. There stood Kintras smiling.

"You know, Kintras, you're right," said Mark, his forehead wrinkled in serious thought. "With the mother I have, I really am blessed."

Kintras was silent for a moment. Then he spoke. "Mark, about the Stone of Rangilor. I have come to ask you for it."

"You want me to give it to you?" asked Mark. He didn't like the idea of giving up Shiner, not with the power it had.

"The Stone is rightfully yours now," said Kintras. "I shall not take it from you by force, but I ask you for it."

"Why won't you take it by force?" asked Mark. "I can't command you. And I know that you are a lot stronger than I am."

"I will not take the Stone because I am not twisted," replied Kintras, looking very grave. "Badrin would take the Stone by force, because he is twisted. But even he would rather acquire the Stone legally."

"Why?"

"My father, Rangilor, made the Stone so that its power to control works only for its rightful owner. If the Stone is stolen or obtained through wrong doing, it will still seek things, but its great power to control will not work."

"Then why did Badrin steal it in the first place," wondered Mark. "Didn't he know it wouldn't work?"

"He knew," answered Kintras. "My father made the Stone at the end of his life and gave it to me. He died before he saw the one flaw in his plan. But Badrin discovered the flaw."

"What is it?"

"Suppose someone stole the Stone," said Kintras, "and threw it into another world, a world in which I have no legal claim. And suppose a citizen of the other world found the Stone. He would, without wrongdoing, become its new owner.

"Then, suppose the thief from my world made his way into the other world and purchased the Stone from its new owner."

"Oh, no!" exclaimed Mark. "Then Badrin would be the rightful owner and Shiner would work for him!"

"Yes," said Kintras, "and he would do great damage in our world, in your world, and in others."

"But couldn't you control him?" asked Mark. "I mean, you caused the piece of wood to rise without Shiner. And you said you can control the 'Twisted Ones' in your world."

"Normally I could control Badrin rather easily by simple commands," agreed Kintras. "And with the Stone of Rangilor, I am hundreds of times more powerful.

"But word has come to me from Tarlis that Badrin has found the Stone of Darkness," he continued. "It is an ancient stone of power created by the first Twisted Ones at the beginning of our world. We thought it was lost or destroyed. But Badrin has found it. With its power Badrin is my equal. If he becomes the rightful owner of the Stone of Rangilor, he will become a hundred times more powerful than I.

"With the power of both Stones, Badrin will do as he pleases," said Kintras. He paused, his eyes grave again. "The fate of the worlds may rest with the decision you make."

"This whole thing gets worse and worse," grumbled Mark. He thought for a moment: double-check your facts!

"I wouldn't sell the Stone to Badrin. Why would he try to take Shiner away from me if it wouldn't work for him?"

"Badrin wanted to take the Stone from you," explained Kintras, "to throw into another world. Perhaps the next person who found the Stone would sell it to Badrin."

"Can't you do something to the Stone?" asked Mark. "I mean, if your father fixed it so that it wouldn't work for anyone but it's owner, couldn't you fix it so that it wouldn't work for bad people?"

"I do not yet have the power to change the Stone," answered Kintras. "My father ruled righteously for a hundred years."

Mark's eyes widened with amazement.

"Yes, Mark," explained Kintras, "the people of my world live longer than your people. Each year that Rangilor ruled and served the Holy One, his power grew. By his hundredth year he had been given enough power to make the Stone of Rangilor.

"I desire the power to change the Stone, to lock it so that Twisted and Broken Ones could not use it," said Kintras. "But I have ruled under the Holy One only ten years. I do not yet have the power to change it."

Both of them were silent as they thought for a moment.

Then Kintras looked keenly at Mark. "You are young," he said, "and I do not wish to frighten you into giving me the Stone. But more lives than your own are at stake in this matter. You must understand the significance of the decision that you are making.

"Take my hand," ordered Kintras, holding out his right hand, "and I will show you."

Mark looked uncertainly at Kintras' hand. Then he cautiously grasped it. Blackness engulfed them immediately.

# The Fate of the Worlds

ARK WAS SO surprised he almost cried out. But he bit his lip and then asked, "What is going on?"

"You will see what things rest on your decision," answered Kintras. "No harm will come to you."

As he spoke, millions of tiny pinpoints of light penetrated the blackness around them. Before them appeared a huge planet which looked like earth. Mark recognized it from the small globe in his schoolroom.

"That is your world," motioned Kintras. "We now stand a thousand miles above it."

Mark stared at the sheer beauty of the planet. North and South America stood out in brown and green against the blue oceans.

"It's beautiful!" exclaimed Mark.

"It is now a battleground between good and evil," replied Kintras. "If Badrin gains the Stone of Rangilor, it will be enslaved by evil. But there is more to see."

Kintras spoke in a language Mark did not understand and signaled with his left arm. As blackness engulfed them again, Mark held tightly to Kintras's hand.

Once more millions of points of light pierced the blackness. Suddenly, before them loomed a bright orange globe with great blotches of green on it.

"Is that another world?" asked Mark.

"Yes," answered Kintras. "It is named Tillith. It has many beautiful deserts as well as many fruitful lands. Watch!"

Tillith traveled toward them at fantastic speed. Then Mark and Kintras plunged feet-first through moist clouds of swirling orange and white.

Mark did not understand exactly what happened after that, but he remembered what he saw.

From instant to instant he looked into the faces of people resembling humans who apparently did not see him: old people, children, men and women, dark-skinned and light; people in crowded marketplaces, in gardens, in homes.

Blackness swallowed them again, and an icy blue planet hung before him. The scenes moved by him more rapidly – people like Kintras at work, at home, alone, in crowds. Always he saw their faces and looked into their eyes.

They disappeared into blackness, and a pale green planet appeared, and then hundreds more faces. World after world sped by. Somehow Mark was looking into the faces of thousands of people at the same time, seeing each one, yet seeing them all at once.

The speed of the images increased until Mark's mind

could hardly keep pace. He felt dizzy.

Then the rush of scenes stopped abruptly. In front of them hung a world covered with blue oceans and large islands colored cream and green. White clouds swirled above it.

"This world will be enslaved, too, Kintras?" asked Mark, turning towards Kintras. He was surprised to see tears in Kintras's eyes.

"No," said Kintras quietly. "If Badrin gains the Stone, this world will be destroyed."

"What world is it?" asked Mark.

"My home," answered Kintras, "Tarlis." Both Mark and Kintras looked at the lovely planet.

Then Kintras spoke again. "On Tarlis we serve only the Holy One. Even with the Stone of Rangilor and the Stone of Darkness Badrin would not be able to make us bow to his evil. So he will destroy us."

They stood in silence. Then Kintras spoke the same strange words and again they were standing behind Mark's barn.

"I will show you more about the power of the Stone, Mark," said Kintras, "but I ask you now to consider giving the Stone to me."

"If I give it to you, what will you do with it?" asked Mark.

"I will command Badrin to be bound and to come to me," said Kintras. "Then I will take him to our world where he will be imprisoned.

"By the power of the Stone of Rangilor I will destroy the Stone of Darkness," continued Kintras. "Then I will rule justly. When I die the Stone will pass to the one of my sons who will rule Tarlis after me. And so the Stone will be passed on until the Holy One closes the ages."

"And if I do not give you the Stone?" questioned Mark.

"Then I shall remain in your world and guard your life," said Kintras. "I will try to prevent the Stone from falling into the hands of a Twisted One. My sons after me shall guard the next person who possesses it, if he refuses to give us the Stone."

"Mark, supper is ready!" Mother called.

"I'll be there in just a minute!" Mark hollered.

"I'd need to talk to my mother before I could give the Stone back to you," said Mark.

"That is as it should be," nodded Kintras.

"After supper I'll tell you what she thinks," promised Mark.

"I shall wait," replied Kintras as he watched Mark walk toward the house.

"And so, I'm going to tell him what you think after supper," Mark finished the story of his meeting with Kintras and their journey through the worlds.

Mother was silent for a few moments, thinking.

"Mark," she said slowly, "I think we should wait until we talk with Dr. Taylor again before we make a decision."

"But Momma, that won't be until tomorrow afternoon!" cried Mark, disgruntled.

"And probably late afternoon at that," said Mother. "But there's an old proverb that says, 'Don't go to war until your advisers agree.' We may indeed be going into war if this Stone gets into the wrong hands. I want the chance to talk with Dr. Taylor once more, just to double-check."

"I understand, Momma," sighed Mark. He paused for a moment, "I wish this whole thing had never happened."

"Well, Mark, there must be a purpose in it. Anyway, through having the Stone at least you got all of the firewood split," she teased.

Mark looked up at her and grinned. "I did, didn't I? I'll

go tell Kintras we are going to wait until tomorrow to decide." Mark laid his fork on his plate, gulped down the last of his milk and ran out the back door.

Kintras greeted him as he came around the barn.

"My mother wants to talk to our friend Dr. Taylor one more time," said Mark, "and he won't be back in town until late tomorrow afternoon. I won't be able to tell you what we will do until then."

To Mark's surprise, Kintras merely nodded, "It is as it should be."

Daylight was fading. In the distance Mark could see the last rays of the sun slipping below Johnson's Ridge. "Where will you spend the night?" he asked.

"In your house. I shall guard you tonight as I guarded you last night, so that no harm will come to you or to the Stone."

"I know you were in my house a little while last night," Mark laughed. "But after you disappeared we searched the whole house and you weren't there."

"I saw you search," smiled Kintras.

"Where were you hiding?"

"Though I am no longer the Stone Master, I am still the ruler of Tarlis. I have the power to create openings between your world and mine. In your bedroom I created an opening and stood in it. You could not see me, but I think your dog could sense my presence. I guarded you until you moved to your mother's room. Then I also moved there and stood guard all night."

"Since you are a ruler, Kintras, don't you have an army? Couldn't you get troops to help you catch Badrin?" wondered Mark.

"One given great privilege must also bear great responsibility," said Kintras. "According to our law, since I was the

Stone Master, the matter is up to me alone."

"And now, young Stone Master," Kintras smiled, "I would like to show you more about the Stone of Rangilor. Remove the Stone from your pocket and put it on the ground beside you."

Mark eyed Kintras suspiciously. "Are you going to try to take it?"

"No," answered Kintras. "All I have told you is true; I am not twisted. I desire only to help you. I will walk away from you, so that you can know for sure."

He walked to the other side of the wood pile.

Mark took out Shiner and cautiously laid it beside his foot. Then he stood up.

"Now, command the Stone to come to you. Say, 'To me, O Stone.'"

"To me, O Stone," Mark repeated. Shiner shot up into his hand. "Wow!" exclaimed Mark. He tried it again with the same results.

"Now," said Kintras, "is there something you wish to remove – something that is a problem, or something that is in the way?"

Mark thought hard for a few moments, then nodded. "Do you see that tree stump behind the barn? The tree died last year, and we cut it down. Mother wanted to plant a small garden in its place but the stump has been in the way."

"Would you like it removed?" asked Kintras.

"Yes," answered Mark, "but big stumps like that one are really hard to pull out of the ground!"

"Hold the Stone of Rangilor in your hand, and picture in your mind the stump completely gone and the ground smooth where it had been."

Mark closed his eyes and concentrated. "I've got it now,"

he said.

"Then command the stump to be unmade," said Kintras.

"Stump, be unmade," Mark commanded. His eyes widened to see what would happen. The air around the stump became "wavy" and shimmered like the air above a hot, paved road on a sunny day.

Suddenly the air cleared, and there was no sign of the stump. Smooth earth was in the place where the stump had been.

"Goodness gracious!" exclaimed Mark. "Where did it go?"

"It no longer exists," explained Kintras.

"This is scary!"

"The Stone must never be used to destroy uselessly," warned Kintras. "But it has the power to destroy."

"Kintras, I have a question," Mark said. "Why are you showing me how to use the Stone? I mean, the more I know about how to use the Stone, the more things I see I can do with it. And the more I see that I can do with it, the harder it gets to give it up."

"I show you these things," answered Kintras solemnly, "because I am not twisted. I would not deceive you."

"The fate of the worlds may rest on your decision," he continued, "but if you give the Stone to me, you are giving up great power. I want you to understand that. You must not give up the Stone out of ignorance or deception. You must give it freely."

"That brings up another question. Why didn't you offer to buy the Stone? Badrin did. From what you said, the Stone would work if it were bought."

The expression on Kintras face became even more serious. "The power of the Holy One should not be bought and sold. As the Holy One gave it freely, so it ought to be given freely. To offer money in exchange for the power of the Holy One is insulting."

"I don't understand," Mark said, puzzled. "I mean, I don't understand what you are saying."

Kintras's stern look softened. "My father walked with the Holy One for years, loving Him and doing His will. Gradually my father was given greater and greater power by the Holy One; the Holy One freely gave it to him.

"The power the Holy One gave my father is now contained in the Stone," he continued. "To try to buy power from the Holy One would insult Him, for He already owns everything. He does not need money. He does not sell, He gives. And what He gives freely should not be sold!"

"I think I see," said Mark, scratching his head.

Kintras smiled. "The Stone could be bought or sold, but it should not be. Some things should never be bought or sold. Love, friendship, the gifts of the Holy One – to offer money for them is insulting."

"Now, for another lesson. Do you see that broken tool?" Kintras pointed to a rusty old axe head lying near the wood pile. Nearly half of the metal head had broken off, and the handle was cracked.

"Yes," nodded Mark. "I broke it last year."

"Picture it as it was when it was new."

Mark shut his eyes and pictured the axe when it was shiny and new.

"Now," said Kintras, "speak to it and tell it to be made new."

"Axe, be made new!" Mark commanded.

For a moment the air around the axe appeared "wavy" like it had around the stump. Then the shimmery air disappeared.

76

There, in place of the old, broken and rusted axe, was a new axe head with a new handle!

"Wow-weee!" yelled Mark, hopping up and down. "Boy! Will this come in handy! Just wait 'til Momma sees this!"

Then he stopped and looked at Kintras. "What all will this work on?" he asked. "Will it work on a house?"

"Yes," grinned Kintras. "To make it new, or to change its color – or to change anything else about it."

"Oh boy!"

"But a word of caution," warned Kintras. "So that others will not ask too many questions, use the Stone only on your own house."

"Can I go show Momma how the Stone works?" grinned Mark.

"You may," nodded Kintras, smiling.

"I'll see you tomorrow afternoon!" called Mark as he turned and ran toward the house.

## The Stone of Darkness

HE NEXT MORNING Mother woke Mark as the first rays of the sun peeped over the horizon. While he pulled on his clothes, Mark breathed in the smells of fresh paint and varnish. Glancing around his room, he admired the new wallpaper, the new, varnished floor, and the fresh paint on the door and trim.

He stepped into the newly wallpapered hallway with its shiny new floors and stairway. As he went down the stairs, something seemed odd. Then he remembered. The third step had always squeaked loudly when he stepped on it. Now it was silent!

And the stair rail felt smooth; there were no nicks or scratches in it! At the foot of the stairs stood Mother, a big smile on her face and eyes sparkling with excitement.

"Let's go outside,"she suggested. "I'd like to see the house from across the street." As they walked through the dining room Mark noticed that the top of the dark mahogany table was smooth and glossy. It no longer bore the scars from years of use.

Like the upstairs, the downstairs was freshly wallpapered and varnished. Even the path worn down the middle of the rug in the parlor was gone! And, the parlor furniture was brand new again.

The brass door knob and hinges on the front door gleamed brightly against the dark varnish on the front door. Mother turned the shiny brass key in the gleaming lock and opened the door.

"The porch no longer creaks!" exclaimed Mother as they crossed it. The outside of the house smelled of fresh paint.

Together they walked down the new, firm front steps and across the road. They stopped and stood looking back at their new house.

"All the trim has been fixed and the roof is brand new!" laughed Mother. "And the new paint is beautiful! It looks just like it did the day your father finished it. He painted it yellow with white and green trim because I love daisies so much!"

Hand-in-hand they walked around the house, admiring the changes. As they passed Trace lying in his doghouse, he lazily opened his eyes, half-heartedly thumped his tail in greeting, then went back to sleep.

The barn had obviously been included in Mark's command to become new. It now stood tall and straight, with a new wood shingle roof and a coat of fresh red paint with white trim.

They walked up the new, sturdy steps to the new back porch, and through the freshly painted back door into the new, fresh white and yellow kitchen.

"It's like a dream," declared Mother. "It looked wonderful

in the dark last night, but by daylight it's just beautiful!

"I'll start breakfast while you make your bed and straighten your room."

"Momma, I just thought of something," Mark said.

"What's that?" she asked.

"What are our neighbors going to think when they see our new house?" asked Mark.

"Well, since we live on the edge of town, it will take a while for the word to get around," she said. She had turned her back to him and was setting the ingredients for breakfast on the gleaming white table beside the stove.

"But what will we tell them when they start asking questions?" wondered Mark.

"I hadn't really thought of that, Mark," she replied absently, setting a new, black iron skillet on the stove. "This new 'old' stove is lovely! It is wonderful to have a stove I have enjoyed so much for so many years and yet have it be brand new!"

Mark could see that she was absorbed in her cooking so he went up to his room.

When breakfast was over and the dishes had been washed in the sparkling white kitchen sink, Mother went upstairs. Mark was wiping off the kitchen table when Randy Starnes came by.

Randy was amazed at the transformation of the house and wanted to know how it had happened. Mark told him it was a secret and that that was all he was going to say about it.

"The supernatural marble?" guessed Randy.

"It's a secret, and that's all I will say," repeated Mark.

Randy was on his way to meet a group of boys who were going to play softball at the schoolyard. He wanted Mark to go with him.

Mark ran upstairs to ask Mother. He promised her he would be on the lookout for Badrin, and would be home by one o'clock for lunch. She gave him permission to go and also to take Trace. She stood on the front porch and waved them off. Mark had his bat over his shoulder, and Trace trotted along behind, eagerly sniffing along the sides of the path.

When they reached the schoolyard, they found a group of men and older boys already playing ball. It would be an hour or so before the ball diamond would be available to the younger boys.

Mark and Randy walked toward the edge of the school grounds where they saw several of the younger boys gathered in a group. Trace happily trotted after Mark. Then the pup saw a group of dogs and ran off to play with them. Mark did not see Trace leave.

As Mark and Randy approached, they could see Leroy Grimes and an older, dark-haired boy at the center of the group.

"There ain't nobody better than Mark Woods when he uses his Shiner!" argued Leroy.

"I don't care if he uses his Whiner!" bragged the older kid arrogantly. "There ain't nobody better than me at marbles! I'm the best there is!"

"Mark's better than anybody 'cause he's got a supernatural marble!" Leroy's face was getting red, and his voice was getting louder.

"I think you've lost your marbles!" scoffed the older boy. "There ain't no such thing as a supernatural marble!"

Mark felt anger begin to surge inside him.

"Didn't you see the Exhibition?" Leroy exclaimed. "We all saw the marble!" The other kids gathering around hollered their agreement.

"I'm new in town," the older kid sneered. "And if you all

saw a supernatural marble, then you're all birdbrains! This town's not only a dump, it's full of birdbrains!"

Mark was mad now.

"Mark's ten times better than you! A hundred times!" yelled Leroy.

"Well, go find your head birdbrain and bring him here," snarled the newcomer. "I can beat him blindfolded!"

"Just try it!" challenged Mark, pushing his way to the center of the group. The other kids cheered.

Leroy stooped down and picked up a small twig. He motioned for the other boys to back up and began drawing a circle in the dirt.

"What are you doin'?" demanded the older boy.

"Making a ring for marbles, dummy!" snapped Leroy. Leroy did have courage – as long as he didn't have to back it up.

"That's for babies and sissies!" denounced the newcomer.

"Well, it don't matter what you play!" said Leroy. "Mark can beat you at anything!"

"What do you want to play, birdbrain?" the older boy asked Mark.

"I'll play anything you can!" Mark's face was red, and his voice shook with anger.

"Stalker!" declared the older boy, smugly. "And for keeps!"

Stalker meant shooting at one another's marbles until one hit the other. Mark liked ring marbles better. But he said, "Okay. Stalker!"

"And for keeps!" said the other boy.

"I don't play for keeps," Mark retorted.

"Then you're a baby, and you ain't got no guts!" accused the newcomer. "Call me when you grow up, and I'll come beat you!" He spat on the circle Leroy had started drawing, sneered at the boys, and swaggered away.

The boys were angry, yelling. Mark's anger boiled over! "Come back, you overgrown chicken!" he yelled. "I'll take every marble you've got!"

The other boys cheered. The newcomer turned around and walked back. He sneered at Mark. "Stalker – for keeps! Agreed?"

"Agreed!" nodded Mark, his voice was quivering with anger. "You first."

The other boys yelled their approval.

The older boy reached into his pants pocket and pulled out a dirty canvas marble bag with a twine drawstring. Reaching into the bag, he drew out a marble that was blue with bands of red, white, and brown.

They were standing near the corner of the schoolyard closest to the town. The older boy shot the blue marble a long way toward the middle of the yard. The marble landed on bare dirt and rolled a bit. Then it curved downhill into short grass. The dark-haired boy grinned nastily at Mark.

"Show him, Mark! Show him!" yelled Leroy and the other boys in encouragement.

Mark pulled the stone out of his pocket.

"It's my favorite!" he said, showing it to the older boy. "I call it Shiner!"

"Shiner, Whiner!" mocked the older boy. "Can you shoot it, birdbrain?"

Mark aimed and shot. Shiner glistened as it flew in a long arc toward the middle of the field. It hit the ground in short grass and began rolling toward the blue marble. The gang of boys ran for the marbles and circled around them.

Mark and the dark-haired boy pushed into the circle at the same time. There was Shiner lying against the blue marble!

Mark picked up the blue marble and held it up in front of the other boys.

"It's mine now," he said with a grin, pocketing the marble.

"Yea! Hooray!" yelled the boys.

"Mark showed you," bragged Leroy, standing almost nose-to-nose with the older boy.

The newcomer pushed him backward. "He was just lucky!" he blustered. "There ain't nobody better than me – 'specially no birdbrain!" He looked at Mark. "You first this time, birdbrain!"

Mark's anger flared higher and his face turned very white. "I'll show you!" he vowed.

He shot Shiner toward the far edge of the yard, the edge that bordered on the woods. Shiner rolled onto a patch of hard-packed dirt without grass.

The older boy reached into his marble sack and pulled out a strange marble. It was black; a deep black so black that it didn't shine, even in the bright sunlight.

The boy had an ugly grin on his face. "This is my favorite," he said. "I call it 'Darkness'!"

The black marble set off alarms inside Mark! He felt he should remember something, but he couldn't put his finger on it.

The dark-haired boy took aim and shot. The black marble flew a long way through the air, hit the ground and rolled swiftly toward Shiner. Plainly, so loudly that all could hear it, the black marble struck Shiner, knocked it several feet, and then rolled up against it again!

"Oh, no!" the boys cried in dismay.

"He won the supernatural marble!" Leroy yelled.

Mark went weak all over. He felt sick. Shiner had a new owner! The Stone of Rangilor belonged to someone else!

The older boy ran from the crowd to get the marbles. He was unbelievably fast. In a second he had scooped the marbles up in his hand. He turned, looked at the crowd of dejected boys and cried, "It's mine! It's rightfully mine!"

He looked at Mark and laughed mockingly. "So long, unlucky boy!" he taunted as he ran toward the woods.

"Badrin!" cried Mark in surprise. "Badrin and the Stone of Darkness!" He took off running after Badrin. "You can't have it!" he yelled. "You can't have it!"

The other boys stood staring, amazed at Mark's behavior.

"Boy! I didn't know Mark was such a sore loser!" exclaimed Leroy as Mark disappeared into the woods. There didn't seem to be much more to say.

"Let's go watch the men's game," suggested Randy after a few moments. They all shuffled toward the ball diamond.

# The Wall of Terror

S MARK entered the woods he ran at top speed through the widely spaced trees, crunching brown leaves and twigs underfoot. Badrin was nowhere to be seen, but his trail was clear. Scuffled leaves with their moist sides now turned up made a dark path for Mark to follow.

"He must run like a deer," Mark said aloud. The trail led across a flat part of the woods for a short distance, and then it angled up the side of Johnson's Ridge. Before long, it merged with a well-worn footpath running along the side of the small mountain.

Mark stopped and studied the path carefully. The damp, turned-over leaves on the footpath indicated Badrin was heading up the mountain. Mark stood listening for any sound of movement. He heard only the wind whispering in the treetops.

Glancing up he saw the high branches with new, green leaves swaying against the blue sky.

Suddenly Mark heard something running through the woods behind him. He wheeled around just as something big and black struck him in the chest! Falling backwards Mark rolled completely over and came up on his knees ready to fight!

In front of him stood Trace, panting, with a big grin on his face. Letting out a sigh of relief, Mark stood up and brushed himself off. Now he smelled like the decaying leaves around him. Slowly his heart settled down. "You really gave me a scare!" he said to the dog, rubbing the coarse hair on Trace's head. "C'mon!"

Mark took off running again, with Trace lumbering along behind him. Mark knew this path. Winding up the mountain side, it finally crossed over the top of the mountain. Near the top of the mountain the path passed by a cave.

Mark ran hard for about ten minutes. He was breathing hard and a pain throbbed in his right side. As he ran, the thousands of faces he had seen with Kintras in the worlds they had visited flashed through his mind. Somehow he had to stop Badrin. He ran on with renewed determination.

Suddenly Trace whimpered uneasily. Mark noticed the woods were growing darker. He glanced up toward the sun. There were no clouds covering the sun, but it didn't seem as bright. That's strange, he thought.

Mark slowed his pace to a jog. As he went up the mountain, the wind blew stronger in the treetops, yet the noise of the blowing wind was lessening instead of growing louder. And the further he went, the darker the woods became.

He stopped and looked around uneasily. All about him hung a pale, gloomy darkness – like the darkness of a winter twilight. He walked back down the trail several paces, and the woods became lighter. He turned around and looked up the trail where the darkness was growing blacker and blacker.

Not sure what the darkness meant, he ran forward again, but at a slower pace. For the first time, he began to think about what he would do if he caught up to Badrin. Since Badrin was the new owner of the Stone of Rangilor, he now had all kinds of power. Who could guess what he might do to Mark! And what could Mark do against the stone?

Trace whimpered again. The gloomy darkness now seemed to be pressing down everything. The woods around him were now as dark as early nightfall. But there were no night sounds – no crickets or night birds, no breeze whispering through the leaves of the trees. Except for the sounds he and Trace were making, everything was deathly quiet, smothered under the blanket of darkness.

Mark walked on. Then without warning, a wave of sadness swept through Mark. It was a depressing heavy sadness which grew desperately intense, then lessened and finally faded away.

Mark felt confused. He didn't really have a reason to be sad. He was sorry Badrin had the Stone of Rangilor, but that made him more angry than sad. And the feeling had come and gone so quickly.

Mark looked over his shoulder. Trace had stopped. "C'mon, Trace!" encouraged Mark. Trace whimpered, then barked. Mark turned and called to him again, and Trace started forward.

A few minutes later sadness returned. He felt as though he were carrying a heavy load on his shoulders. The sadness grew deeper, and Mark felt a great weariness pulling him down on the inside. A lump formed in his throat, and he almost burst into tears. Then, quickly, the wave of emotion left.

Mark continued up the trail trying to figure out what was happening. Why should he be feeling sad? Again the deep, deep sadness came. Only this time it came in big waves, swiftly welling up inside him. Mark felt he had lost all that was dear to him. Grief gripped his insides: stabbing sadness made him want to scream and wail! He burst into tears, but kept on running.

Finally, the grief became so intense his insides felt tied in knots! He bent over, holding his cramping stomach, crying. For a moment he had trouble getting his breath. Trace looked at him curiously, tilting his head from one side to the other. Then the intense feelings disappeared.

Mark straightened and wiped the tears from his face with both hands. Pulling his handkerchief from his rear pocket, he blew his nose loudly. The intense feelings confused and frightened him.

He tried to pull his thoughts together. It seemed that as the darkness increased, the waves of sadness worsened. Something was affecting his mind and feelings. He didn't know how much more he could stand, for the last wave of grief had bent him double.

Mark decided to fight the sadness. He would try keeping his mind on his mother and how happy she had been when she saw the new "old" house.

"Let's go boy!" he said to Trace. As he moved on through the darkness he remembered the delight on Mother's face when she had seen the new kitchen. He could picture the smile on her face and her brown eyes glowing as she saw the old stove gleaming like new.

All of a sudden the delight on Mother's face turned to horrible, wrenching grief! Mark saw her kneeling over his own lifeless body, screaming and crying!

A deep, uncontrollable grief swept over Mark! Tears poured down his face and his breath came in great gasping sobs. The stabbing pain of grief was intense, but Mark gritted his teeth and kept running.

And then, fear struck. The grief faded as a creepy, prickly feeling tingled up Mark's spine and a chill ran through his body. He sensed something waiting for him in the darkness ahead: something big and ugly – something deadly! He shivered. Had he heard something? He thought he had heard what sounded like rough breathing. What was out there?

Mark stopped and looked quickly around. He desperately wanted to turn around and run the other way, but he knew he had to find Badrin. Gathering his courage, Mark trudged through the growing darkness. In a moment the fear lessened and then faded quickly until it was gone. Mark was relieved but still uneasy.

A minute later sheer panic struck. The hair on Mark's arms and the back of his neck stood up. His heart pounded fiercely. There, directly in front of Mark in a small clearing, stood Badrin. A pale blue light lit the woods around them.

Mark halted. Trace stopped beside him, growling.

Badrin held something in his right hand. He grinned wickedly at Mark as he raised his hand and spoke in a strange language. A sullen, black cloud as large as a house appeared beside Badrin. It quickly sank down to the ground where it began to shrink, becoming solid as it grew smaller.

Where the cloud touched the ground, four black paws as big as washtubs appeared. Above the paws the cloud swiftly condensed into legs shaped like a dog's but as thick as a man's waist. The cloud continued to shrink, forming the body and tail of a monstrous black dog as tall as an elephant!

Pointed ears took shape; then red, flaming eyes. Even

before the long, slender muzzle was completely formed, Mark knew he was standing face to face with a gigantic wolf!

The huge beast snarled at Mark, its white fangs glistening against its red tongue and black fur. Then it lunged!

Mark tried to run but his legs wouldn't move! Just before the wolf reached Mark, its lunge was stopped short by a black chain around its neck. The wolf threw back its head and howled in fury, straining against the chain fastened to a huge stake in the ground.

For a moment the wolf stopped and stood still, its flaming eyes intent on Mark. Then it lunged again. Savagely it fought the chain, snarling, barking! Mark wondered how long the chain would hold!

Again the wolf stopped, panting. Then it crouched at the end of the chain, ears laid back and fangs bared. Its red, wicked eyes fixed on Mark as it started licking its slavering jaws.

Badrin walked over to Mark with a coil of rope. "Oh no, you don't!" cried Mark. He started to raise his arms to fight Badrin, but they wouldn't move!

With an evil smirk on his face Badrin pushed Mark over backwards and tied the rope around his ankles. Then he walked back to the wolf, trailing out the rope behind him. He stood beside the wolf and began pulling Mark quickly toward the snarling beast.

The monster opened its mouth to tear into Mark's legs! Then suddenly Badrin and the wolf were gone! Mark realized that he was standing in the dark, silent woods alone, his arms and hands free. He could feel his heart racing, and his palms were sweaty. He bent over with his hands on his knees, taking deep, calming breaths. He wasn't sure what had happened, but at least it was over. The whole thing must have been some kind of dream or vision.

The paralyzing panic evaporated, but the prickly feelings remained. Mark looked around for Trace and called, but he was nowhere to be found. It couldn't be much farther to the top of the mountain, he thought.

Mark started forward again – but halted two steps later. A few inches in front of his nose and nearly invisible in the darkness, was a tall, wide wall of wavy air. He edged closer to the wall and looked at it carefully. The waviness apparently extended high into the trees and stretched into the woods on either side of the trail.

The only other times Mark had seen "wavy" air was when he had used the Stone to work on something. Was Badrin now working in this part of the woods with the Stone?

Mark stuck his left hand into the wavy air. It felt deathly cold. Although he could still see his hand, it looked distorted, as if he were seeing it through an old window pane. But Mark could not see what lay on the other side of the waviness.

Mark took a deep breath and plunged into the distorted air. Suddenly grief and panic both attacked him! In front of him he saw his mother kneeling over his torn body, screaming and sobbing hysterically. From the wild look on her face he knew that her grief had driven her crazy. He saw men in white coats take her arms and drag her away. Her desperate screams tore through his heart. If only he had run home instead of into the darkness!

Mark jammed his hand into his mouth and bit it to keep from screaming. The pain from the bite cleared his head. The vision of his mother and of his dead body disappeared – as did the grief and panic.

Mark took another step forward through the wall of shimmering air. His legs and feet now moved with difficulty, as though he were walking through deep thick mud. The next moment he felt the shock of heart-breaking grief. All around him he heard screaming and wailing, like the cries of people desperate and without hope. Mark put his hands over his ears, but the wailing grew louder.

Then, in front of him stood the great black wolf. And this time there was no chain on it!

## Desperate Plans

ERROR SEIZED Mark. He wanted to run, but his legs would not move. His arms and legs were paralyzed. He closed his eyes, but it did no good. Even with his eyes closed, he could still see the beast!

For a second the gleaming red eyes of the wolf studied him. Then with ears laid back, it bared its fangs and growled ferociously. Its huge jaws gaped, and the wolf stepped forward and bent down to take Mark in its teeth! Mark felt its stinking breath hot on his face. With a crunch the beast sank its teeth deep into his flesh! Searing pain shot through his arm and shoulder.

Mark opened his mouth and screamed in agony, but no sound came out. He felt lightheaded and sick at his stomach. Was he going to faint? He desperately longed to pass out to escape the horrible pain!

Then the wolf let him go and raised its head. Its long tongue licked the bright red blood off its black muzzle.

Mark fell to the ground. In agony he glanced down at his mangled shoulder and arm. Blood flowed from dozens of large holes. He strained to move his limbs but they didn't respond.

The wolf bent down, terrible teeth bared, ready to bite into him again!

It only tasted me the first time, Mark thought in terror. Now it's going to eat me alive!

Mark strained to move! Suddenly his arms and legs were free! Struggling to his feet, he spun around to run.

From behind him came a blinding burst of pure, beautiful silvery light. Mark turned back and watched in astonishment as the powerful light shone through the wolf like the light of a lamp through its shade. The beast melted away into nothing! The surrounding woods were lit by the mysterious light.

Mark turned toward the light and took a slow, difficult step forward. Another step brought him out of the wavy air. He could now walk without difficulty. As he stood in the light Mark realized he no longer felt pain. Looking down at his wounded arm and shoulder, he saw no blood or teeth marks! His arm and shoulder were perfectly normal!

The whole experience had not really happened! Mark wondered if the dark, shimmering wall of wavy air had something to do with the sadness and the terrifying visions he had experienced.

For a moment the silvery brilliance lit the trees ahead like the glow of a great fire, casting shadows. Voices like those of Badrin and Kintras came from a short distance in front of Mark. One voice talked loudly and excitedly.

The light dimmed to a soft luster, glimmering in the

darkness ahead. Now and again flashes of silvery light shot into the woods at random, like someone flashing a search-light beam.

Moving as quietly as he could, Mark started toward the light. He was now nearing the clearing at the top of the mountain. On one side of the clearing was the cave. The trail ran between it and the cliff.

Mark tried to think of a plan. He could rush in, knock the Stone of Rangilor from Badrin's hands, then grab it and run away into the darkness! Badrin might chase him, but Mark knew the trail and the mountain well. He could easily hide in the darkness.

For a moment Mark liked the plan. Then Mark remembered. Since Badrin was the new owner, he could call the Stone back to himself. Badrin also had the Stone of Darkness. Mark wasn't sure what its powers were, but Badrin could probably use it to find Mark or hurt him!

He would have to hide in the bushes and when Badrin came near, bash him in the head with a rock! If Badrin was unconscious, he couldn't use the Stones. Mark could then grab them and escape. Maybe he could find Kintras.

The plan was a desperate one, and he knew it. It could easily fail. Maybe Badrin really would create a giant wolf to eat him alive, and Momma would be brokenhearted. He knew she already carried grief inside her because of his father's death. She might grieve so much that it would kill her!

Sadness started rising up again in his heart. Then he saw his own torn, lifeless body lying in front of him. Panic raced through him! Mark bit his hand again. The vision dimmed, and the feelings faded with it. Though he was through the wall of darkness, apparently he wasn't completely safe from the visions.

Mark knew that somehow he had to keep control of himself, or his thoughts and emotions would run away with him! He remembered Dr. Taylor's advice: pray for wisdom, keep a pure heart, and double-check your facts!

Mark prayed for wisdom. Then he thought about what was going on inside himself. It was fear! He prayed for courage. Then he thought about the facts. He remembered the worlds and the people Kintras had shown him. He might indeed die if he went after the Stone, but who knew how many millions would die if he didn't!

A feeling of calm came over him. Whatever the terror, whatever the grief, whatever happened he knew what he had to do.

As he approached the clearing, he scanned the trail for a good rock to use on Badrin. A few feet ahead he saw one about the size of a brick and picked it up.

Soon he was at the edge of the clearing. Someone was talking very loudly. Mark moved quickly, hoping the loud voice would cover any noise he made.

Leaving the trail, he moved toward mouth of the cave. He quietly worked his way through the bushes growing beside the entrance. In a few moments, he carefully parted some branches and peeped into the clearing. His eyes opened wide.

A few feet away, with his back to the mouth of the cave, stood Kintras!

Mark started to call out but checked himself. Kintras was poised and alert, staring straight ahead with a look of intense concentration and determination on his face.

About twenty feet in front of the cave, facing Kintras, stood Badrin! Shafts of silver light poured from the closed fists of Badrin's left hand, streaming through gaps between his fingers. As he talked, Badrin shook his fist at Kintras, flashing silvery light in all directions. The beams were small but extremely bright, lighting up the clearing.

Badrin's face was twisted with hatred and mockery. He spoke in a loud, scornful voice. "You fool!" he scoffed. "Through the opening in the cave I shall enter my first world to conquer it, and you cannot stop me! You are powerful, but I am more powerful. The Stone of Rangilor is mine!

"Stand aside! I am ready to taste my destiny as Ruler of the Worlds. Get out of my way!"

"You will not enter the dark opening!" refused Kintras firmly, not taking his eyes off Badrin's face.

"I do not want to kill you yet!" yelled Badrin, frustrated. He began to walk back and forth in front of Kintras. "I want you to wait in dread until I come to Tarlis to destroy you. I want fear to eat its way deep inside you. I want you to taste terror before I come to unmake you. So stand aside, or I will destroy you now!"

"I do not fear you," declared Kintras firmly. "I fear only the Holy One."

"So! You are arrogant in the face of death!" mocked Badrin. "I could make another opening here beside me, but I will not give you the satisfaction of knowing you blocked my way. Move, or I shall destroy you now. I have both the Stone of Rangilor and the Stone of Darkness."

"Darkness has no power over a servant of the Holy One," said Kintras. "Even the darkness you created to dim my power has not harmed me."

"True, true," agreed Badrin, as he paced in front of Kintras. "But with the Stone of Rangilor I can destroy you!" He laughed a wicked, taunting laugh.

Kintras said nothing. Badrin's black eyes flashed with anger and hatred as he motioned for Kintras to move. "Stand aside, or I shall kill you now!"

"If my body dies, I will step into the presence of the Holy One," declared Kintras. "I will not fear you!"

"Then you will die!" screamed Badrin, shaking his right fist at Kintras. Badrin stopped his pacing and stood directly in front of Kintras. He straightened his shoulders.

"As Ruler of the Worlds, my first act is to destroy the ruler of Tarlis," he announced majestically. "Tarlis is now mine – and so are the other worlds! Even the Holy One will not stand in my way, for now the Stone of Darkness and the Stone of Rangilor are both mine!"

"You do not know the Holy One," said Kintras. "Even the very plan you make for conquest will become the path of your own defeat!"

"Do I look defeated?" laughed Badrin. "The Stone of Rangilor is mine, fool! And my first act as its rightful owner is to destroy you, my enemy."

"If you are not defeated in Tarlis or in any of the worlds, you will still be destroyed when the Holy One ends the ages," predicted Kintras.

Mark was amazed at Kintras' calm.

"Fool!" yelled Badrin. "By the power of the Stones I will prevent the ages from ending." Badrin raised his arms and stretched them out toward Kintras. He clenched the Stones in his fists. Then he spoke loudly and solemnly, "By the power of darkness," he shook his right fist, "and the power of your father's own work," he shook his left fist, "I will now destroy you!"

Kintras stood quietly facing Badrin, his hands at his sides. Mark watched in horror.

"I have it in my mind now!" cried Badrin with excitement. He drew a deep breath to say the words of destruction.

"No!" screamed Mark as he burst through the bushes into the clearing. He threw the rock as he ran, but it fell short of Badrin. Badrin was startled and lowered his arms slightly. Mark ran to Kintras' side. Kintras turned, his clear, blue eyes looking deep into Mark's eyes.

"I couldn't bear to see you die alone!" said Mark, tears streaming down his cheeks.

Kintras didn't say anything, but he put his right arm around Mark's shoulders and hugged him tightly against his side. Together they faced Badrin.

"Foolish boy!" scoffed Badrin. "Now I shall destroy both! Think of it! Destroying two Stone Masters with one command," Badrin bragged. "Worthless brat! You should have taken the gold and troubled me no more. You would have at least lived out your days."

"But the Stone isn't rightfully yours," accused Mark. "You cheated!"

"How so?" asked Badrin, an arrogant look on his face. "My plan was perfect. I told you no lies: I was new in town. We contracted a wager. It was supernatural stone against supernatural stone. I helped you get angry – but that is your problem, not mine. Servants of the Holy One should learn to keep their tempers under control," he mocked.

"But you were seen by a whole crowd of boys,"argued Mark, "and it is forbidden for you to be seen by more than one!"

"Ah," jeered Badrin. "You have become an expert on the law of Tarlis! But I violated no law; I was in disguise."

At the mention of the word "disguise" Mark's heart sank. He remembered.

"Am I not correct, ruler of Tarlis? Or former ruler, I should say," Badrin taunted.

"It is true," answered Kintras. "We can be seen by many if we are in disguise."

"I have it in my mind now!" said Badrin. "Two former Stone Masters exploding into nothing!" He laughed wickedly. Again he clinched the Stones in his fists and raised his arms, stretching them towards Mark and Kintras.

Mark knew this was it! Kintras stood calmly, looking Badrin in the eye. Mark gritted his teeth and closed his eyes. His heart pounded terribly. In his mind he saw worlds and their people; they would all be slaves! And Tarlis would be destroyed. And Mother . . . .

"Be unmade!" commanded Badrin in a loud voice.

# The Dagger's Work

ARK DIDN'T FEEL anything happen. He wondered if that was how it felt when you were unmade – you didn't feel anything.

"Be unmade !" This time Badrin's voice was more of a shriek.

Mark opened his eyes to see Badrin shaking his fists furiously.

"Be destroyed!" Badrin screamed. Something had obviously gone wrong!

"Perhaps your plan was not as perfect as you thought, Twisted One," said Kintras. "When one twists himself, he twists not only his heart but also his mind."

The Stone of Rangilor flashed beams of light as Badrin shifted the Stones to opposite hands and stretched his arms out toward them again. "Be unmade!" he screamed.

"You mentioned a wager, Twisted One," reminded Kintras.

"Yes! And it was agreed upon and fairly won!" said Badrin hotly.

"Mark," said Kintras, still looking at Badrin, "are wagers legal in your world?"

"In some areas they are," Mark answered.

"What about in this area?" asked Kintras.

"No," replied Mark, "all betting is illegal."

"Then call the Stone of Rangilor to you, Stone Master!" cried Kintras.

Before Mark could think of what to say, Badrin had dropped the Stone of Darkness and pulled out a dagger. "You will die first!" he screamed angrily. The dagger flew through the air as Badrin spoke!

Kintras jumped in front of Mark, and the dagger sank deep into his chest! Kintras fell to the ground and lay with blood flowing freely from the wound. Mark froze in horror.

"Call the Stone!" gasped Kintras.

"To me, O Stone!" yelled Mark.

Badrin screamed, trying to hold onto the Stone with both hands! But it burst out of his grip with a blinding flash of light and flew to the hand of its rightful owner. Mark held the Stone so that its light flooded the clearing.

Badrin stepped back and and picked up a giant rock, lifting it over his head. He swung it back to throw at Mark.

"Be paralyzed!" commanded Mark.

The rock dropped harmlessly to the ground as Badrin's body went stiff! He fell backwards like a tree, arms stretched rigidly over his head. He lay on the ground, screaming with rage.

"Be silent!" Mark ordered. Badrin lay mute, mouth open

in a soundless scream.

Kneeling beside Kintras, Mark began to cry. Kintras raised his hand, and Mark grasped it. Kintras squeezed Mark's hand tightly. "The Stone of Darkness!" he whispered, his eyes wide with pain. "Call it! Destroy it! Do not touch it!"

Mark closed his eyes, and thought of the Stone of Darkness lying beside him. "Stone of Darkness, lie by my side!" Mark commanded. The Stone of Darkness swiftly flew from the other side of the clearing and lay several inches from Mark's left leg.

Kintras turned his head to watch. Even though Mark was not touching the Stone of Darkness, a dark, thrilling, wicked feeling poured into his lower leg. The feeling rose swiftly past his knee into his thigh as though it was flowing in his blood.

"Destroy it – quick!" Kintras urged.

"Be destroyed!" shouted Mark. The Stone of Darkness rose high into the air above Mark's head, swelling and growing as it lifted. With a thunderclap it exploded into a cloud of swirling, absolute blackness.

The dense blackness swirled round and round, spinning and whistling as it grew until it became a roaring storm engulfing Mark, Kintras – everything. With the screaming winds of blackness came a piercing, suffocating odor like rotten eggs.

In his right hand Mark tightly gripped the Stone of Rangilor. Looking through the thick, swirling darkness, he could see only a faint glimmer of the light from the Stone. All else was utter blackness!

Holding Kintras's hand tightly, Mark bent over his body to protect him. Bowing his head to the roaring winds, Mark closed his eyes against the flying dirt and sticks. He coughed, struggling to breathe. The winds of darkness howled and beat against him fiercely!

Suddenly, the fury of the winds lessened. Mark opened his eyes. He could see his hand again by the light of the Stone. The foul odor was fading. In another second the wind calmed, and the light from the Stone pierced the darkness around them.

Mark looked up and saw a great ball of blackness spinning above the clearing! The wind within it whistled shrilly as the blackness rapidly shrank. As the ball dwindled to the size of the Stone of Darkness, the whistle became an ear-splitting, high-pitched whine. Then with a pop, the ball of blackness was gone!

High in the air, where the Stone of Darkness had been, a loud sucking noise began and grew louder. The gloomy darkness of the clearing started moving round and round in a great circle, slowly at first, and then faster and faster.

By the light of the Stone, Mark could see the darkness swirling thicker and blacker above him. Like water being sucked down a drain, the darkness drained with a roar from the forest into the "nothingness" where the Stone of Darkness had been. In a few moments the last of the darkness disappeared into the "nothingness," and all was silent and still.

Sunshine filled the woods around Mark and Kintras. A timid chirp came from a nearby tree. Then all around birds began to stir in the trees. One bird burst into song. Others joined it.

The Stone of Darkness was no more!

"Command . . . a servant of the Holy One . . . from Tarlis . . . to appear," gasped Kintras.

Mark looked down at Kintras. Blood trickled from the corner of his mouth. Kintras lifted his head up slightly from the ground. There was pain in Kintras' eyes, but he smiled as he looked up at Mark.

"Well done, Stone Master," Kintras smiled. "I die . . . in

peace." Kintras's head fell back to the ground. His hand went limp in Mark's.

Mark gently placed Kintras's hand beside his body. Then he buried his face in his hands and wept bitterly! If only he hadn't gotten so angry at the school yard, Kintras would be alive! If only he hadn't become so proud and tried to show up the dark-haired boy!

Dr. Taylor's words came back to him: "Your enemy will easily trap you!" Pride! He had fallen right into Badrin's trap! And it had cost Kintras' life!

Mark ached on the inside. As the tears flowed, Mark began to hate himself. For a long time, he sat beside Kintras's body and cried. Then he remembered that Kintras had told him to call for a servant of the Holy One. Badrin also might have friends. Mark looked around. There was no one near.

Gripping the Stone of Rangilor, Mark declared, "I command a servant of the Holy One from Stargis-Lin of Tarlis to come to me !"

Immediately there stood before him a little man who looked like Kintras. He, too, had golden hair and deep blue eyes, and wore a green garment trimmed with gold.

He first glanced at Mark, then spied Kintras. Kneeling beside Kintras's body, he looked up at Mark.

"Are you the new Stone Master?" he asked as tears filled his eyes.

"Yes," replied Mark, with tears welling up in his own eyes again.

"Have you killed my brother?" the little man asked.

Mark started to cry again. "I didn't . . . kill him," he sobbed. "*He* did," Mark said, pointing toward Badrin. The little man turned and saw Badrin lying on the ground. Then he stood up, wiping tears from his eyes.

"I am Klostin of Stargis-Lin, second son of Rangilor, brother of Kintras. It is now my duty to guard your life and to guard the Stone. How may I serve you?"

Mark regained control of himself. "Before he died, Kintras said to call for a servant of the Holy One. I thought you would know what to do."

"On your command," said the little man, "I will take Badrin to Tarlis. In Stargis-Lin, the capital city, he will be executed, for he has now murdered.

"I will also take my brother's body back to Stargis-Lin for burial according to the honor due him."

"Badrin threw the dagger at me. Kintras stepped in front to save me."

"Then my brother has died with even greater honor than he had while he lived," declared Klostin. He bowed his head and was silent for a moment, tears flowing down his face. Then lifting his head, he spoke, "I will finish the business in Tarlis quickly and return to guard your life."

Something was nagging at Mark's mind. "Don't go yet." Mark blurted. "Let me think a moment."

"I shall wait," nodded Klostin.

Mark thought. Pray for wisdom; he did. Pure heart? Mark knew it wrong to hate himself so he decided to stop. Double-check the facts . . . . An idea came into his head.

"Klostin," he said, "by Kintras's help I made an old, rusted axe new. Then I made a house and barn new. Can the Stone of Rangilor make a person new?"

"I do not know," answered Klostin slowly. "It has not been tried. And I do not know if it is permitted."

"Is it forbidden?"

"No. Perhaps it would be more accurate to say it has not been considered."

"Then I shall try," decided Mark. He stood over the lifeless body of Kintras and held the Stone in his right hand. Then, raising his right arm straight up toward the sky, he prayed for a moment. Next he thought of how Kintras was before the dagger was thrown. He licked his lips; his mouth felt dry.

Klostin stood watching expectantly.

"I now have Kintras in my mind," said Mark. "Kintras, I command you, be made new!" Mark almost shouted, hoping the extra volume would help.

Then he stared wide-eyed at Kintras's body. The air all around it became "wavy"! Mark could make out Kintras's form inside the wavy space, but it was impossible to see exactly what was happening.

Though it couldn't have been more than a minute or two, it seemed that the air shimmered forever! Then the waviness began to fade. Mark closed his eyes, afraid to look.

"Hail Stone Master!" said a familiar voice.

Mark's eyes popped open! He saw Kintras lying on the ground, smiling up at him! There was no dagger, no wound. Tears of joy streamed down Mark's face.

"Kintras!" he cried, kneeling down beside him. "Are you okay?"

"This is indeed a wonder!" exclaimed Kintras. "A moment ago I was talking with my father, and now I am here again!"

"Hail, Blessed of the Holy One!" greeted Klostin, grinning.

Kintras saw his brother. "Klostin! So you're the one who came!" Kintras leaped up and the two brothers embraced, clapping each other on the back and laughing.

Suddenly Mark thought of the time and remembered his promise to Mother. "Oh, no!" he exclaimed. What time is it?"

"In the time of your old world it is a bit after one o'clock," answered Klostin.

"I told Mother I'd be home by one o'clock. And it will take me more than an hour to get there! She will be worried!"

Kintras grinned and pointed to the Stone, "The Stone of Rangilor will take you there immediately when you command it. Klostin and I will take Badrin to Tarlis. Then I will return to you and await your answer regarding the Stone."

Kintras and Klostin picked up Badrin like two men lifting a small log. The air around them became wavy. Suddenly Mark was alone in the woods.

Gripping the Stone tightly in his right hand and sticking his hand into his pants pocket, he pictured himself standing on the front porch of his house. "To my home, O Stone!" he commanded.

Immediately he was standing on his front porch! Trace was at the side of the house barking up into a tree. On one of the lower limbs sat a gray cat.

Trace spotted Mark and came running. He bounded up onto the porch and jumped into Mark's arms! Mark was ready this time. He caught the big pup and Trace licked his face. "Some guard dog you are!" laughed Mark as he hugged Trace. After a final rub of his ears, Mark put Trace down.

He ran to the front door and opened it. The aroma of fresh bread greeted him.

"Is that you, Mark?" Mother called from the kitchen.

"Yes, Momma!" he answered as he ran toward the kitchen. "Boy, have I got something to tell you!"

# The Return

HEN MARK burst into the kitchen he was surprised to see Dr. Taylor and Mrs. Taylor sitting at the table. Mother was taking a pan of bread from the oven.

"Hi, Dr. Taylor, Mrs. Taylor," Mark called out. "Hello, Mark," grinned the doctor. "I'm back a bit early. I finished my work in Riverport sooner than I expected, so we came by to catch up on the news." He took a sip from a glass of water beside him.

"What do you have to tell us, honey?" Mother asked. She was emptying pinto beans into a bowl. When she turned to put the beans on the table, she saw Mark's face. "Why Mark! You've been crying!"

"Yes, Momma. For a while things were so terrible! But now, they've turned out so good!"

"Tell us about it, Mark," requested Mrs. Taylor.

Mark and his mother sat down at the small table, across from the doctor and his mother. The food remained untouched while the adults listened intently to the story of the marble game and the battle in the woods.

When Mark finished, Mother put her arm around him and pulled him close. She put her head down on top of his and held him tightly for a few moments. Then she straightened and smiled. "Let's talk this over while we eat," she suggested.

Dr. Taylor led in prayer. Then they filled their plates and started eating. Mark was starved! The adults asked him a few questions, but mostly they talked while he ate. Mark was first to finish his meal.

They all agreed the Stone of Rangilor should go to Kintras.

"He's the original owner," said Mother.

"He obviously is not twisted, like Badrin," added Dr. Taylor.

"And it sounds like their world really needs the Stone," commented Mrs. Taylor.

"Other Twisted Ones will probably come after it if we keep the Stone here," pointed out Mother.

"And, I'm afraid I would do something really stupid with all that power," said Mark. "I've already wanted to use it to show off. I know Kintras wouldn't do dumb things with it."

"I think the sooner the Stone is given to Kintras the better," suggested the doctor.

"I agree completely, Mark," nodded Mother.

"Then may I be excused?" asked Mark. "I want to go see if Kintras is back."

"Oh, Mark," said Dr. Taylor with a slight smile. "Before you go, tell me, do you admire Kintras?"

"Do I!" said Mark, his eyes shining. "I sure do!"

"Do you admire him because of his great wealth?" the doctor asked.

"No, I hadn't really thought about his money."

"Do you admire him because of his powers?"

"No," said Mark slowly, thinking. "I think that, with Shiner, I have as much power as he does – maybe even more."

"Do you admire him because he is a king or a ruler of a world?"

Mark was silent for a moment and then shrugged, "I haven't thought that much about him being a king."

"Then why do you admire him?" the doctor asked.

Mark thought a moment. "Because he is good," he answered. "And he does good to people. He likes seeing good things happen to them. And because he's brave to do what is right. No matter what it costs him, he does what is right."

Mark paused for a moment, "And because he died to protect me," he added. He looked up at Dr. Taylor. "I think those are the big things."

"Now, tell me something else," said the doctor, leaning forward slightly. His blue eyes were deep and penetrating. "For what do you want to be admired, Mark?"

Mark dropped his eyes for a few moments and stared at his empty plate, thinking. "I see what you mean," he said sheepishly. "I wanted people to think I was something because I had a magic marble. But I admire Kintras because of the kind of person he is."

Mark raised his eyes to the doctor's. "I'd like to be admired for the same kinds of things, sir," he said.

Dr. Taylor stretched across the table and put his hand on Mark's shoulder. "And so would I, son," the doctor added quietly. He squeezed Mark's shoulder and then smiled. "Go and find Kintras."

Mark ran out the back door. Trace heard the door slam and came running around the corner of the house. He followed Mark to the side of the barn where he stopped.

As Mark rounded the corner of the small barn he heard, "Hail, Blessed of the Holy One!" It was Kintras's voice, but there was no sign of Kintras! Mark scanned the woodlot again.

"Kintras!" laughed Mark, "Where are you?"

"Here!" Kintras's voice came from immediately in front of Mark. A moment later he stepped out of nowhere and stood in front of Mark. Trace, peeking around the corner, growled at Kintras.

"You stood in an opening!" exclaimed Mark.

"Yes," Kintras grinned.

"Where is it?" Mark asked.

"There," said Kintras, turning and pointing behind him. "If you look closely, you will see a faint disturbance in the air."

Mark stepped forward and looked hard at the air in front of him. He shifted his eyes from side to side, trying to see the opening. There it was!

"I see it!" he cried. "It's wavy, like the air around some-thing when the Stone is working. And like the air around you and Klostin when you left the woods with Badrin."

"Yes, " replied Kintras, "that is it. They are hard to see unless you know what to recognize."

"And on the other side of the wavy air is Stargis-Lin?" asked Mark.

"A few steps away," smiled Kintras. "Perhaps one day the Holy One will grant that you go there."

"You read my mind!" accused Mark with a laugh. Then he asked, "Badrin – is he in jail?"

Kintras's face became grave. "The law of Tarlis requires the life of a murderer," he said quietly. "Badrin has faced his punishment."

Mark was a bit shocked that Badrin had been dealt with so speedily. Kintras seemed to read his mind again. "In Tarlis, justice comes quickly, for the law is not twisted and those who judge are not twisted. And, upon command, even those who twist themselves must tell the truth."

They were both silent for a moment. Then Kintras spoke. "A great celebration has begun in Tarlis," he said. "A celebration of the victory over darkness. For days there will be feasting, music and songs. Klostin is overseeing the festival. I have returned to guard you, Stone Master." He smiled again.

"Oh, I came to tell you," remembered Mark. "We have decided to give the Stone of Rangilor to you. We think it should really belong to you."

"Then we will celebrate both the return of the Stone and the locking of the Stone."

"What do you mean, 'the locking of the Stone'?" asked Mark.

"You know that I have wanted power to change the Stone so that the Twisted Ones could not use it, reminded Kintras.

"Yes," said Mark.

"I have wanted to lock the Stone so that danger to the worlds could be avoided. But I thought it would take a hundred years or more to gain enough power to lock the Stone."

"And it won't?" Mark asked, his eyes wide.

"Though I have reigned only ten years, I now have more power than my father did at the end of his reign," said Kintras. There was no pride in his voice.

"Where did you get it?" asked Mark.

"It seems to have come when I saved your life by giving up my own," replied Kintras. "When you renewed me, I came back more powerful than I ever dreamed of being. So now I have the power to lock the Stone."

Mark thought for a moment. Then he pulled Shiner out of his pocket. He held it in his open palm in the afternoon sunlight. Rainbows of color danced on the side of the barn. "I guess I'll never have another marble like this," he sighed.

"That is true," agreed Kintras. "But, now you want to be admired for more than marbles, right?" Kintras grinned, "I overheard the conversation."

Mark smiled back. He held out his open hand with Shiner in it. Kintras stretched out his hand toward Mark to receive the stone. When he did, Trace started barking at him.

Kintras laughed and squatted down on the ground. "Come!" he said to Trace. The pup came closer, moving cautiously at first. Then he trotted over to Kintras and stood calmly beside him. Kintras petted Trace's head, and Trace licked his hand.

"I think we can proceed now," said Kintras, smiling as he stood.

"I, Mark Woods, the Stone Master, give the Stone of Rangilor to Kintras of Stargis-Lin of the world Tarlis, eldest son of Rangilor, elder brother of Klostin," Mark announced. That sounded official enough to him.

"And I, Kintras of Stargis-Lin, receive the Stone of Rangilor," declared Kintras. "To me, O Stone!"

The Stone lept from Mark's hand to Kintras's palm.

"Hail, Stone Master!" saluted Mark, grinning.

"Thank you, Mark," said Kintras earnestly. "Although you have some ideas of the greatness of the good you are doing as you return the Stone to me and my people, it is still a far greater good than you realize. On behalf of my world, I thank you."

"You have given the Stone freely," Kintras continued.

"So now I shall give to you freely: I shall refresh your mother! In two days time, money from the sale of some gold from a certain chest will be deposited in the bank in your mother's name. The money will not make her rich, but together with her job, it will make a good income for the two of you."

"I don't mean to be ungrateful, Kintras," said Mark, "I am really glad for the gift. But, why won't you make us rich?"

Kintras smiled. "Because it is very hard for a Broken One to use that kind of power without doing something foolish."

Mark laughed. "I can understand that!"

"I must return now to Tarlis, to my people, my wife and family," said Kintras. "There I will lock the Stone of Rangilor. And then we will build a memorial to you, your mother, Dr. Taylor and Mrs. Taylor for the great kindness you have done in returning the Stone."

"I wish I could see it," said Mark wistfully.

"Then tonight as you dream in your sleep, you shall," replied Kintras.

"And will I be able to remember it when I wake?" asked Mark hopefully.

"If you wish," answered Kintras, "I will make it so."

"Oh, one more thing," said Mark with the same tinge of hope in his voice.

"Yes?" asked Kintras, a smile spreading across the face.

"Could Mother and Dr. Taylor and Mrs. Taylor see the memorial and remember it, too?" Mark asked.

"It will be done," agreed Kintras.

"Mark!" It was Mother calling. "Mark!"

"Yes, Momma!"

"I have some cake and milk ready in the kitchen!" she called.

"I'll be there in just a minute!"

Mark and Kintras looked at each other in silence.

"Will I ever see you again, Kintras?" Mark asked, his voice quivering slightly and tears welling up in his eyes.

"Yes, Mark," answered Kintras gently. "I do not know where or when. But I do know that we shall meet many more times before you have lived out your years."

Kintras embraced him and then stepped back, smiling. "You and I both have good news to carry to our people." With a wave he stepped back and disappeared. Mark looked hard at the place where Kintras vanished. He could see the faint waviness of the opening to Tarlis.

"Until we meet again, Blessed One!" called Kintras' voice, with a hint of laughter in it.

"Until then, Stone Master!" laughed Mark, waving. He turned and ran back to the house with Trace bounding at his heels.